The Ballad of the False Messiah

Also by Moacyr Scliar:

The Centaur in the Garden
The One-Man Army
The Carnival of the Animals
The Gods of Raquel

Cover design by Bill Toth

Book design by Iris Bass

Author photograph by Stephen Fischer

The Ballad of the False Messiah

MOACYR SCLIAR

Translated by
Eloah F. Giacomelli

AVAILABLE
PRESS

BALLANTINE BOOKS • NEW YORK

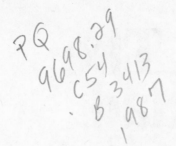

An Available Press Book

Copyright © 1987 by Moacyr Scliar

All rights reserved under International and Pan-American Copyright Conventions. Published in the United States of America by Ballantine Books, a division of Random House, Inc., New York, and simultaneously in Canada by Random House of Canada Limited, Toronto.

Library of Congress Catalog Card Number: 87-91480

ISBN 0-345-34904-0

Manufactured in the United States of America

First Edition: November 1987

THE BALLAD OF THE FALSE MESSIAH

HE'S ABOUT TO POUR THE WINE INTO THE GLASS. HIS hands are now wrinkled and unsteady. And yet, those big, strong hands of his still deeply affect me. I compare them with my own hands with their stubby fingers and I admit that I've never understood him and never will.

I first met him on board the *Zemlia*. We were Jews leaving Russia in that old ship; we feared the pogroms. Enticed by the promises of America, we were now journeying toward our destination, crammed into the third class. We wept and were seasick in that year of 1906.

They were already aboard the ship when we embarked. Shabtai Zvi and Natan de Gaza. We shunned them. We knew that they were Jews, but we from Russia are wary of strangers. We dislike anyone who looks more Oriental than we do. And Shabtai Zvi was from Smirna, in Asia Minor—one could tell by his swarthy complexion and dark eyes. The captain told us that he was from a very wealthy family. As a matter of fact, he and Natan de Gaza occupied the only decent stateroom in the ship.

1

What made them then leave for America? What were they escaping from? Questions with no answers.

Natan de Gaza, in particular—a short, dark-complexioned man—roused our curiosity. Until then we had never seen a Jew from Palestine, from Eretz Israel—a land which to many of us existed only in dreams. Natan, an eloquent public speaker, would tell an attentive audience about the rolling hills of Galilee, about beautiful Lake Kineret, about the historical city of Gaza, where he had been born, and whose gates Samson had wrenched off their hinges. When drunk, however, he would curse his native land: "Nothing but rocks and sand, camels, larcenous Arabs . . ." When we were off the Canary Islands, Shabtai Zvi caught him execrating Eretz Israel. He beat Natan up, until he collapsed on the floor, where he lay bleeding; when Natan dared to protest, Shabtai knocked him out with one final kick.

After this incident he spent days shut up in his stateroom, speaking to no one. As we walked past his door, we could hear moans . . . and sighs . . . and melodious songs.

One day at dawn we were awakened by the shouts of the seamen. We rushed to the deck and saw Shabtai Zvi swimming in the icy sea. A lifeboat was lowered and with great difficulty he was pulled out of the water. Stark naked as he was, he walked past us, without a glance in our direction, his head held high—and he went straight to his stateroom, where he shut himself up. Natan de Gaza said that the bathing in the sea had been an act of penance, but our own conclusion was quite different: "He's crazy, this Turk."

We arrived at Ilha das Flores in Rio de Janeiro, and from there we traveled to Erexim, from where we proceeded in covered wagons to our new homes in the settlement called Barão Franck, named for the Austrian philanthropist who had sponsored our coming. We felt very grateful to this man, whom, incidentally, we never met. It was rumored that later a railroad would be built across the lands where we were being settled, and that the baron was interested in the valuation of the shares of stock in the railroad company. I don't believe this rumor was true. I do think that he was a generous man, that's all. He gave each family a plot of land, a wooden house, agricultural tools, livestock.

Shabtai Zvi and Natan de Gaza stayed with us. They were given a house, too, although the baron's representative wasn't pleased with the idea of having two men living together under the same roof.

"We need families," he stated incisively—"not fairies."

Shabtai Zvi stared at him. It was such a powerful gaze that it froze us.

The baron's agent shuddered, bid us farewell, and left hastily. We threw ourselves wholeheartedly into our work.

How hard country life was! Felling trees. Plowing the fields. Sowing . . . Our hands were covered with bleeding blisters.

We hadn't seen Shabtai Zvi for months. He had shut himself up in his house. Apparently he had run out of money because Natan de Gaza began to wander about the village, asking for clothes and food. He would tell us that Shabtai Zvi would reappear in the near future to bring good tidings to the entire population.

"But what has he been doing?" we would ask.

What has he been doing? Studying. He has been studying the Cabalah, the masterpiece work of Jewish mysticism: The Book of Creation, the Book of Brightness, the Book of Splendor. The occult sciences. Metempsychosis. Demonology. The power of names (names can exorcise demons; a person well-versed in the power of names can walk on the water without getting his feet wet; and there is also the

power of the secret, ineffable, unpronounceable name
of God). The mysterious science of letters and
numbers (letters are numbers and numbers are letters;
numbers have magical powers; as for letters, they
are the steps leading to wisdom).

It is around that time that the outlaw Chico Devil
puts in an appearance at Barão Franck for the first
time. A fugitive from the law, he comes from the
frontier, he and his band of desperados. While
fleeing from the "Stetsons," he finds a hideout near
our settlement. And he plunders and he destroys
and he sneers. Laughing, he kills our bulls, wrenches
out their testicles, then eats them slightly roasted.
And he threatens to kill every one of us if we
denounce him to the authorities. As if this misfortune weren't enough, we are struck by hail, which
destroys our fields of wheat.

We are plunged into the deepest despair when
Shabtai Zvi reappears.

He is transformed. Fasting has ravaged his once
robust body, his shoulders stoop. His beard, oddly
turned grey, now reaches down to his chest. Saint-
hood enfolds him like a mantle and it glows in his eyes.

Slowly he walks toward the end of the main
street . . . We drop our tools, we leave our houses, we
follow him. Then, standing on a mound of earth,
Shabtai Zvi addresses us.

"Divine punishment will befall you!"

He was referring to Chico Devil and to the hail.
We had attracted God's wrath. And what could we
do to expiate our sins?

"We will abandon everything: the houses; the
cultivated fields; the school; the synagogue; with our
own hands we will build a boat—the timber of our
houses will be made up into the hull, and our
talliths will be made up into sails. Then we will cross
the ocean. We will arrive in Palestine, in Eretz
Israel; and there, in the ancient, holy city of Sfat, we
will build a large temple."

"And will we await the coming of the Messiah there?" somebody asked in a trembling voice.

"The Messiah has already come!" shouted Natan de Gaza. "The Messiah is right here! The Messiah is our own Shabtai Zvi!"

Shabtai Zvi opened the mantle which enveloped him. We stepped back, horrified. What we saw was a naked body covered with scars; circling his belly was a wide belt studded with spikes that penetrated his flesh.

That day we stopped working. Let the hail destroy the cultivated fields. Let Chico Devil steal our livestock; we no longer cared, because we were leaving soon. Jubilant, we tore down our houses. The women sewed pieces of cloth together to make sails for the boat. The children gathered wild berries to make jam. Natan de Gaza collected money, which was needed, he said, to buy off the Turkish potentates that ruled over the Holy Land.

"What's been going on in the Jewish settlement?" wondered the settlers in the neighboring areas. They were so intrigued that they sent Father Batistella over to find out. The priest came to see us; he was aware of our plight and willing to help us.

"We don't need anything, Father," we replied with great earnestness. "Our Messiah has come; he's going to set us free and make us happy."

"The Messiah?" The priest was astonished. "But the Messiah has already been here on earth. He was our Lord Jesus Christ, who changed water into wine and who died on the cross because of our sins."

"Shut up, Father!" shouted Sarita. "The Messiah is Shabtai Zvi!"

Sarita, the adopted daughter of fat Leib Rubin, had lost her parents in a pogrom. Ever since, she had been mentally unbalanced. She would follow Shabtai Zvi everywhere, convinced that she was destined to become the wife of the Anointed of the Lord. And to our surprise, Shabtai Zvi accepted her; they were married on the day when we finished the hull of the boat. As for the vessel itself, it was quite good; we planned to transport it to the sea on a big oxcart, the way Bento Gonçalves had transported his own boat.

There weren't many oxen left. Chico Devil was now showing up once a week, each time stealing a couple of them. Some of us began talking about confronting the bandits. Shabtai Zvi disapproved of this idea. "Our kingdom lies overseas. And God is protecting us. He will provide for us."

Indeed: Chico Devil disappeared. For two weeks we worked in peace, putting the finishing touches to the preparations for our departure. Then on a Saturday morning, a horseman galloped into the village. It was Gumercindo, Chico Devil's lieutenant.

"Chico Devil is ill!" he shouted without dismounting from his horse. "He's seriously ill. The doctor doesn't seem to be able to come up with the right treatment. Chico Devil has asked me to bring your saint over so that he can cure him."

We surrounded him in silence.

"And if he refuses to come with me," Gumercindo went on, "then I have orders to set the whole village on fire. Did you hear?"

"I'll go," thundered a strong voice.

It was Shabtai Zvi. We made way for him. Slowly he drew closer, his eyes fastened on the outlaw.

"Get down from the horse."

Gumercindo dismounted. Shabtai Zvi mounted the horse.

"You go in front of me, running."

The three of them set off: Gumercindo, running ahead; then Shabtai Zvi, on horseback; and bringing up the rear, Natan de Gaza, riding on a donkey. Sarita wanted to go with them, but Leib Rubin didn't let her.

We were assembled in the school building all day long. We were far too anxious to speak. When night

fell, we heard a horse's trotting. We ran to the door.
It was Natan de Gaza, gasping for breath.

"When we got there," he said, "we found Chico
Devil lying on the floor. Beside him, a witch doctor
was performing his sorcery. Shabtai Zvi sat down by
the bandit. He didn't say a word, he didn't do a
thing, he never touched the man—he just sat there
watching. Then Chico Devil raised his head, looked
at Shabtai Zvi, let out a yell, and died. The witch
doctor, he was killed right then and there. I don't
know what happened to Shabtai Zvi. I came over to
warn you: Cut and run!"

We got into our wagons and fled from Erexim.
Sarita had to be taken forcibly.

On the following day, Leib Rubin called us to a
meeting.

"I don't know about the rest of you," he said, "but
I've had enough of the whole shebang: Barão
Franck, Palestine, Sfat. . . . I've made up my mind to
go to Porto Alegre. Do you want to come with me?"

"And what about Shabtai Zvi?" asked Natan de
Gaza in a shaky voice (was he feeling remorse?).

"The hell with him. He's nuts!" yelled Leib Rubin.
"He has caused us nothing but misfortunes."

"Don't speak like that, Father!" shouted Sarita. "He
is the Messiah!"

"The Messiah, my foot! Enough of this story—it's
the kind of thing that might well provoke the
Jew-haters. Didn't you hear what the priest said? The
Messiah has already come, didn't you hear? He
changed water into wine, among other things. And
we're leaving. That husband of yours, if he's still
alive—and if he has gotten his head together—can join
us later. It's my duty to look after you—which I'm
going to do, husband or no husband!"

We traveled to Porto Alegre. Kindly Jews took us
in. And to our surprise, Shabtai Zvi showed up a
few days later. The "Stetsons," who had arrested
Chico Devil's gang, brought him to us.

One of the soldiers told us that they had found Shabtai Zvi sitting on a stone, his eyes fixed on the body of Chico Devil. And throughout the floor—the bandits, dead drunk, lay snoring. There were quartered oxen scattered everywhere. And wine. "I've never seen so much wine! Every single container previously filled with water was now filled with wine! Bottles, flasks, buckets, basins, barrels. The waters of a nearby marsh were red. I don't know if it was the blood of the oxen or if it was wine. But I think it was wine."

With the help of a wealthy relative, Leib Rubin set up shop: first he ran a store that sold fabrics. Then he moved on to furniture, and eventually he established a brokerage firm, and ended up amassing a great fortune. Shabtai Zvi worked in one of his companies, where I was also an employee. Natan de Gaza, after getting mixed up in some smuggling activities, had to flee the country and was never heard of again.

After Sarita's death, Shabtai Zvi and I got into the habit of getting together in a bar to drink wine. That's where we spend our evenings. He doesn't say much, and neither do I; he pours the wine and we drink in silence. Just before midnight he closes his eyes, lays his hands over the glass and murmurs some words in Hebrew (or in Aramaic, or in Ladino). The wine is changed into water. The bar owner thinks it is just a trick. As for myself, I'm not so sure.

DON'T RELEASE THE CATARACTS

I AM A GOD OF JUSTICE. EVEN FROM THE INSIDE I can look and see: A bus runs across the hollow of the night. The lakes reflect the pale Moon. Men murmur.

It is fair: The lakes have been placed there so that they can reflect the pale Moon and so that men, touched by the sight, can murmur: "The lakes reflect the pale Moon." Everything has been planned from the beginning in the fairest possible way. Many remain unaware of such eternal designs: They open highways, and set buses to run on them. Where are they going in such a hurry? I know. They don't. Yet they keep running.

The passengers are asleep. All except for one. A short, thin man; he is forty years old, has worn a mustache for twenty years and bifocals for ten years.

He boarded the bus in Porto Alegre. He said good-bye to his wife and children; he was quitting his dull job; he was flying the coop. He thought that nobody knew about it. I know.

"In Florianópolis I'll have dinner at Aurora Restaurant. In Florianópolis I'll make new friends. In Florianópolis I'll have a mistress." He was chuckling

to himself. They are funny: They come up with
phrases, then they laugh. The little man laughed a
great deal. But time went by. And now he sits
wriggling. It's funny. He wriggles like an earthworm.
And he screws up his face. He is no longer laughing.

Three times already has he reached out for the
buzzer. But he hasn't pressed the button. Because he
knows that pressing it would be useless.

There are men who can cut short the course of
events by merely pressing a button. He is not such a
man: The bus driver has already told him that he can't
stop. There is a pregnant woman on the bus, he has
to reach Florianópolis without delay so that the child
can be born on terra firma. Clever, this bus driver.
He knows that the baby will be a leader and that the
little forty-year-old man is already in the death
throes—already rotten, maggoty. He stinks. He has
some kind of disease, and he stinks of ammonia.

The passenger, however, thinks otherwise. "It's not
fair the way I'm being treated," he whimpers. It is
fair, yes: I am a god of justice. "I've paid for my bus
ticket, I have rights. . . ." There are no rights, my
dear fellow; only concessions. The owner of this bus
line has a concession: He has been granted the right
to put buses without toilets on the Porto Alegre–
Florianópolis run. You have a different one: You've
been granted the right to whimper. Until the moment
of the ultimate silence.

He suffers, this man, bloated up that he is, like a
pregnant woman. Suffering takes the joy away from
this trip; he even feels half-dead. . . . What does he
expect me to do? Let him find support in recollect-
ing his friends, his mistress, Aurora Restaurant.
(Ineffective crutches, aren't they, my cripple?)

"Why? But why?"

So much anxiety. Well, I'll reply then. In the
beginning, a hollow seed was sown in his lower
belly. It was named bladder. Centuries and hours
have gone by, and the bladder fills up: It's a

pouch—elastic, true, but only up to a point. It
contains lukewarm urine. In a moment the man will
have the Sun in his belly. "How it burns!" However,
as it is said in the psalm, neither the Moon at night
nor the Sun in the daytime should burn him—far less
so this Sun of the night.

Sweet memories come to the man's mind: "How
good we felt in that public urinal! All of us, citizens
of Porto Alegre. Some would chat, others would
whistle, many would compare sizes. We would
watch the yellow rivulets run along the little white-
tiled canals, heading toward the bigger river."

And where do you think the bigger river flowed,
my friend?

Nothing escapes my control. Nothing. Every one
of those men who stood chatting or whistling or
comparing sizes will have to account for everything.
For every single droplet of urine.

The man is anguished, afraid he's going to die. He
looks at his watch: I see that his time hasn't come
yet. Therefore, I take pity on him. And I decide to
come to his rescue: I allow him to notice an empty
bottle on the seat next to him.

He looks at the bottle. Listlessly, at first, stupefied
as he is by suffering. Gradually he begins to show
an interest in the bottle. Then he sets his brains to
work. Zoom . . . the bus runs. The man thinks and
thinks. In a scientific way: hypotheses, calculations.
He imagines that he is plotting his own fate. That's
all right. He has my permission to think in this way.

Even from the inside I can look and see. I see him
unzip his fly, I see him relieve his bladder. The
urine pours out into the bottle. Aaaah . . . such a
beautiful song.

This orgasmic act lasts a few seconds, and then is
over. And as soon as it is over, the man has already
forgotten the past suffering, it's completely out of his
mind! He sticks his head out of the window, sees
lights in the landscape of Santa Catarina state, and

feels cheerful: "I've been born again!" It's a lie. He was born only once, forty years ago. And he will die at the age of forty. Only once. I am a god of justice. Each person gets one chance.

He presses the bottle of urine, still warm, against his chest. Quite understandable it is, this tenderness surfacing in the middle of the night: After all, it is his own urine. Nothing could be more his in this world. A moment of tenderness . . . But so fleeting. He is already rejecting his own liquid: Filled with disgust, he opens the window and hurls the bottle up into the sky; the bottle turns a somersault in the air. For a moment the drops sparkle in the moonlight. Then they are swallowed by the black earth.

The bus runs on.

But the seeds have been sown. In that place, in that earth, poisonous mushrooms will sprout, the kind of mushrooms that incurably poison the kidney. Mushrooms. Which a farmer will pick, then sell to the manager of Aurora Restaurant.

And who will eat them? Hm, who will eat them?

I am tired. In Florianópolis I will take a long, long rest. It is only fair: I am a god of justice. My name is Kidney.

NEW YEAR, NEW LIFE

LIFE IS PAIN, AND I WAKE UP WITH A TOOTHACHE. IT'S
a gorgeous day, a summer sun invades the shack; as
for myself, I'm crying with pain. I'm crying for
other reasons as well, but mostly, I'm crying with
pain.

Life is a fight. It's no use lying down. I get up and
start exercising. While flexing my torso, I notice
Francisca's note lying on the chair.

Writing is one of Francisca's latest achievements;
with great sacrifice, she attends a literacy course in
the evenings. Her handwriting has been improving by
the day, as I verify when I unfold her message,
which unfortunately doesn't give me any further
reason to feel pleased: Francisca has just left me for a
longshoreman—as a matter of fact, her choice matches
her lack of sensitivity perfectly well, but it also
creates problems for myself: Who's going to do the
cooking? Who's going to tidy up the shack? Who's
going to get me money for the movies? Alas, life is
worries.

But life is also joy. The Sun shines, the physical
exercises do me good, and if Francisca ditched me,

13

well, there are plenty of other women for the asking.
Actually, I bear Francisca no grudge. She has never
measured up to me. Because, if nowadays I live in a
shack, it's by choice: I was raised by a rich uncle, I
never lacked the necessities of life, but I suffered from
boredom. It was boredom that turned me into a
hippie. Later I decided to turn professional and I
became a genuine destitute man. That's what brought
me to this shack, where I lived by myself at first; later
Francisca, at the time a domestic servant who didn't
know how to read or write, moved in with me. And
now she has ditched me. Ah well, it doesn't matter;
onward, I say, tomorrow will be another day.

The toothache, momentarily eased, is back with a
vengeance. I'll have to see a dentist, I conclude.
White rum with tobacco won't do me any good,
especially because—in this case—there isn't any
white rum or tobacco around. In times like these I
rather regret having left my uncle's house. At least,
I shouldn't have discarded the credit card that he had
given me.

I decide to go to the dentist at the village's benevo-
lent association—he treats the poor free. The dentist
turns out to be a nice fellow, chubby and likable; after
a quick examination, he decides it's a case of
extraction. I have a choice, he informs me: either
extraction with anesthesia (which will cost me a
modest sum of money), or without. I opt for the
latter, and I howl when the tooth is pulled out. The
dentist thinks that I scream with pain, but he's wrong:
it's a howl of satisfaction with having saved money.
To spend money to make me insensitive? How
absurd. Life is suffering; to suffer is to swig life
down, I explain to the dentist when I take my leave,
my mouth full of blood.

Spitting out globules of blood upon the dusty roads
of the village, I head for the city center with the
intention of having some coffee, since I didn't have

any morning coffee, might as well have some afternoon coffee: it's almost three o'clock.

I am surprised by the hustle and bustle downtown. Large crowds of people in the streets, in the stores. Suddenly it dawns on me: It's December 31. The last day of the year!

Life is emotion. I recall how my uncle and I used to celebrate the end of the year: with cakes and champagne aplenty. Uncle, I forgot to mention, was an importer of fine wines, so the champagne was always of the best quality, but even so it was rather difficult for me to get stoned with him. The night of December 31 was a night of dreams and hopes. Remembering this, I sit down on the curb of the sidewalk and cry and cry. . . .

Hunger stings me. I stand up, ready to battle with life. Life is a battle.

I devise a plan: I set forth clearly defined—and ambitious—objectives: I'll manage to get hold of some money, I'll buy champagne and cakes, I'll celebrate New Year's fittingly. My uncle would have no cause to feel ashamed of me.

But what about money? Where can I get it? Not knowing very well what to do next, I begin to stroll along Rua de Praia, hoping that something will turn up. Something does turn up: At the corner of Rua da Praia and Rua Uruguai I run into the dentist. I accost him, and ask this compassionate man for a loan. Much to my surprise, he refuses; he pushes me aside, he wants to be on his way. Desperate as I am, I grab him.

"Keep your hands off me, you bum! Why don't you get a job, you good-for-nothing!"

He extricates himself free and walks away, muttering. I let him go: His wallet is already in my hand.

Chortling, I step into a dark recess and examine the fruit of my labor. In addition to a credit card, I find a one-hundred cruzado bill. Happy New Year!

I enter a confectioner's shop to buy cakes. As I'm taking the wallet out of my pocket—a blow on my hand! A purse-snatcher! I've been robbed!

I leave the store in hot pursuit of him: *Thief! Thief!* During the chase we run past the dentist, now also following hot on our heels: *Thief! Thief!* I keep running, hoping that the dentist is with me, not against me.

Finally, a policeman cuts short the race of the pickpocket. I thank the cop and ask for the wallet back. Unfortunately, the dentist has now caught up with us and is also demanding the return of the wallet. The credit card settles the matter. If only I hadn't discarded mine. . . .

My mouth starts bleeding again, which is unpleasant, but it gives me an idea: I head for a hospital with the intention of giving blood. I've heard that they pay well.

The doorkeeper won't let me in.

"I've come here to give blood," I explain.

"You?" He laughs. "You look as if you badly need a transfusion yourself."

Night has already fallen when I return to my shack: with no cakes, with no champagne, with nothing. Life is wretchedness.

Seated on the bed, I weep. And then I recall the dentist's advice, and I start the New Year with a resolution: I'll work.

I'll plant a grapevine. All I need is one grape, one single grape from which to take out the seed. In a few years I'll have a vineyard and then I'll be able to make my own champagne. New year, new life: tomorrow I'll get hold of one grape.

THE SCALP

A FAMILY—FATHER, MOTHER, DAUGHTER—WAS TRAV-
eling by car through the hinterland. The father, still
young, was an engineer; he was driving in a bad
mood because it was hot; besides, the generator was
malfunctioning. His wife, who was pregnant, was
fanning herself with a paper fan. His daughter—a
five-year-old girl—was lying asleep on the back
seat. Throughout the preceding kilometers she had
been acting up, crying, and biting her mother. Now
she was asleep.

The car, an old Ford, advanced with difficulty
along the muddy road, which was flanked with
steep banks of red earth rising on either side. The
engine was groaning, the water in the radiator was
boiling. The engineer was beset with anxiety. Night
was beginning to fall and he was afraid that the
engine might conk out. Cursing under his breath, he
kept pressing down the accelerator.

All of a sudden the woman let out a cry: "Look,
over there!" Startled, he braked the car: "What is
it?" "Over there," she said, "right in front of us." A
young woman was walking along the road. Tall,

with a beautiful body. Her naked feet were kneading
the mud of the road. "But what's the matter?"
asked the husband, puzzled. "Her hair," murmured
the wife, "how beautiful her hair is!"

Slowly they drove past the young woman, who
turned around; smiling, she stood staring at them
for a long time.

The wife sighed, and fidgeted on the seat. "Stop
the car," she groaned. The engineer slowed down:
"Aren't you feeling well? Do you want to throw up?"
She lowered her eyes: "No, I don't want to throw
up; it's something else, but I'm not telling you
because I know you won't do it. . . ." "What is it?"
asked the engineer. She, tearfully: "It's no use telling
you, you won't oblige me. . . ." "But what is it
that you want?" Worried, the husband glanced at his
watch. "Out with it, for heaven's sake!" She blew
her nose: "That woman . . ." "Yes," said the engineer, "that woman; what about her?" "Have you
noticed her hair?" The wife was no longer crying;
her eyes were now glistening. "What about her
hair?" groaned the engineer. "Come on, tell me, what
about her hair?" "Black," replied the wife, "black
like mine, but much longer, far more beautiful."
"Yes," said the husband, "so what? What's the
problem?"

"Nothing," said the woman, lowering her head. A
large teardrop gathered on the tip of her nose.

The engineer stared at her, bewildered. "So, shall
we press on?" he asked. "Wait," she murmured,
and noisily blew her nose. "But can't you see," he
shouted, "that it's getting late, that we still have
another sixty kilometers of this dreadful road ahead of
us? Do I drive on or not?" She raised her head, took
a deep breath, and said angrily: "All right, drive on,
let's go. And let's drop the subject, okay?"

He stepped on the brake pedal, turned off the
engine. "No, now you've got me worried, I want
you to tell me what's the matter with you." The

wife, silent. The young woman with the black hair
came into sight, overtook them, smiled again, and
walked on.

"Her hair," said the woman. "But for God's sake,
what about her hair?" shouted the engineer. "People
buy it," the wife shouted back. "People buy it—
didn't you know? People buy it! To make wigs! It
costs a fortune in the city. Here, you can get it
cheap."

The engineer was staring at the young woman,
who then disappeared around a bend of the road. "I
gather that you want to buy her hair," he said in a
low voice. "No," said the wife with a smile, "I
want *you* to buy it. It's going to be a gift from you."

"No way," muttered the husband, turning on the
engine. With a beseeching smile, she rested a hand
on his arm: "Please, darling."

"Okay," he sighed. He drove off.

They overtook the young woman. The car came to
a halt and the engineer got out.

"Good afternoon, young lady," he said with a
forced smile. "Good afternoon," she replied; gorgeous, she was; her teeth were in pretty bad shape,
but her eyes were beautiful, and such hair! Long,
black, falling over her naked shoulders. The young
woman looked at him, waiting.

He explained: He would like to buy her hair to give
it to his wife, many girls sold their hair, didn't she
know? Yes, she did, the young woman knew about it
but she couldn't sell her hair. She had promised her
dying mother: She would only cut her hair when she
had her own man. "Whoever gets my hair gets me
as well," she said, crossing herself. The engineer still
tried to persuade her to change her mind; seeing that
it was pointless to persist, he thanked her and went
back to the car. "She won't sell it," he said to his
wife.

"That's a lie," shouted the wife, her eyes glittering
with anger, "she'll sell it all right, they all do, she's

just trying to raise her price." "Maybe," said the
husband, turning on the engine, "but we're driving
on." "No!" shouted the woman, her face distorted by
pain. "Please!"

The engineer—*oh God, I sure got out of bed on the
wrong side today*—turned off the engine and got out
of the car.

The young woman had left the road and was now
walking along an uphill trail. He followed her.

She walked at a brisk pace. He was trying to
overtake her, he got scratched in the shrubs. He was
panting. Insects buzzed. . . .

He overtook her in a glade, where she had stopped
to take a rest.

"Young lady," he murmured.

She turned around. She didn't seem surprised. She
was smiling.

"Young lady, see, it's like this: My wife is pregnant, she mustn't get upset, you understand, don't
you? Do sell me your hair, young lady," he said.

"It's impossible," she was saying with a smile,
"I've already told you I can't sell my hair." She
stood up and disappeared amid the trees. He hesitated
for a moment, then cursing, went in pursuit of her.
His boots sank into the damp earth, sweat ran down
his neck. He overtook her once more. "Young
lady," he groaned. She stared at him, saying nothing.

He cut off her hair while still lying on top of her.
In a rage, he cut it off with his knife, a fistful at a
time. She didn't make a single gesture, didn't say a
single word. She kept staring at the treetops.

He ran back to the car, stumbling over roots. He
opened the car door, flung the strands of muddy hair
at his wife: "There you are, hold on to them."
"How disgusting," protested the woman, "you've

dropped the hair, haven't you?" "Yeah," he said,
and drove off. "It's all right, I'll have it washed," she
said after considering the matter. She carefully
placed the hair into a plastic bag.

Kilometers farther down the road, the engineer
touched his shirt pocket with his hand: He had lost
his documents. But I'm not going back there, he
said to himself, nothing in the world will make me.
The child woke up: "What's that, Mother?" "It's a
wig for Mummy," the mother intoned. "Give it to
me," whimpered the girl. "Shut up," the father
yelled. Both mother and daughter shut up.

The wig was made, months went by, a child was
born—a boy.
    One Sunday afternoon the engineer was relaxing at
home, reading a magazine. He was alone. His wife
and children had gone out for the day.
    The bell rang. He got up with a groan and went to
the door.
    It was the young woman. Her hair hadn't grown
back yet; her smile was the same.
    "Remember me?" she said, and stepped in.

THE SPIDER

MOTIONLESS ON THE WHITE WALL—THE SPIDER.
The legs, eight of them, are articulated to her black
body. The spider has been there for a long time.
Waiting: the male will soon be there.

At the moment, he is away on a hunting expedition. He is after flies; pouncing upon them, he kills
them, then draws nourishment from their delicious
juices. Soon he'll forget their depleted carcasses.
He'll return to the female. The killing has roused him:
He wants to copulate.

Their legs entangled, they make love. Then they
disengage themselves. While he lies, lethargic, she
moves away a little. Then suddenly she is back,
energized—with a quick, accurate maneuver she
pulls out one of his legs. And then devours it with
pleasure: it has the taste of a dry, velvety cracker.
The male, gripped by a sudden dread, wants to flee
but can't: deprived of the support of his limb, he
heels over, out of control. On the white wall, the
female makes periodic raids on the male and
dexterously extracts leg after leg.

Finally, all that is left of him is his trunk, from

which every outgrowth has been excised—and yet,
fits of spasm still ruffle his coat. What is left of him is
so small that the she-spider—with only a minor
effort—could gulp it down in its entirety. Which she
does. Then she remains motionless on the white
wall of the spacious bedroom: she and Alice.

Lying in bed, Alice only noticed the spider at the
moment when she stretched her long, brown leg.
Alice had been gazing at herself; it wasn't until her
eyes roamed beyond herself that she caught sight of
the spider. Her first impulse was to squash it to death.
But she didn't want to soil the wall. She lay staring
at the spider.

Alice was waiting for Antonio. Soon he would be
there after leaving the grocery store; late, as usual,
he would come huffing and puffing: "I'm much too
fat to be climbing these stairs!" To make up for it:
rings, earrings, cold cash. And a fur coat, too: "How
do you like this beast?" He would notice the spider
on the wall: "An insect!" A blow with the flat of his
huge hand—and there: A black smudge on the wall.
He would wipe his hands on his pants, and then
would lie down on the wide bed.

For the time being, the spider remained alive. And
motionless. She didn't even stir when the key
turned in the lock, or when the voice thundered: "I'm
much too fat to be climbing these stairs!" He was
huffing and puffing, Antonio was. With a smile, he
held out a package wrapped in newspaper. "A
surprise! Made them myself. A recipe from the old
country!" Alice opened the package: dry crackers.
Made in various shapes: snakes, lizards. Alice took a
cracker out of the package. "A spider!" shouted
Antonio. Alice bit into a leg: dry, velvety. Slowly,
she crunched it. Dark crumbs fell upon the white
bedspread, but she wasn't looking at them.

She was looking at Antonio. Naked, he was slowly
drawing near the wall, his raised hand splayed.

Alice slid down to the floor. On all fours on the

carpet, she advanced noiselessly and more quickly than the man. Antonio came to a halt, ready to deliver the blow. As for Alice, she saw a hairy leg in front of her. She bit into it. Caught unawares, the man let out a yell. Alice bit again. The leg wasn't dry: it was fleshy, it bled.

With a kick, Antonio shoved her away. He was swearing at her loudly while he put on his clothes. Finally, the door slammed shut. Silence fell upon the bedroom.

Alice smiled. And she stood staring at the spider, motionless on the white surface.

AGENDA OF EXECUTIVE
JORGE T. FLACKS FOR JUDGMENT DAY

*S*EVEN A.M.

Get up (earlier, today). Don't think. Don't
lie motionless in an attempt to recapture fleeting
images; let dreams trickle away, jump out of
bed.

From the terrace: watch the Sun rise—with dry
eyes, without thinking of the millions, billions of
years throughout which this poignant light, and so on
and so forth. Nothing of the kind. A bath, soon
afterward.

Seven-thirty A.M.

Breakfast: orange juice, toast, eggs. Eat with appe-
tite, chew vigorously and swiftly; don't ruminate,
don't mix food with bitter thoughts. Don't! Coffee.
Very strong, with sugar today, just today, never
again (from now on, avoid expressions such as
"never again"). Finish off the meal with a glass of
ice-cold water, sipping it slowly. Pay special attention
to the ice cubes tinkling against the glass. Joyful
sound.

Eight A.M.

Wake up the wife. Make love. And why not? She's been the companion of so many years. Wife, mother. Make love, yes, a quick act of love, but with the utmost tenderness. Let her go back to sleep afterward. Let her roam through the country of dreams as much as she wants; let her say farewell to her monsters, to her demons, to her fairies, to her princesses, to her godparents.

Eight-thirty A.M.

Gymnastics. Brisk, fierce movements. Afterward, feel the arms tingling, the head throbbing, splitting, almost: life.

Nine A.M.

Take the car out of the garage. Drive downtown. Take advantage of the time spent driving to do some thinking. Try to clarify certain doubts once and for all; maybe stop off at the rabbi's place. Maybe talk to a priest as well. Maybe bring priest and rabbi together?

Ten A.M.

At the office. Render decisions on the latest documents. Tidy up the desk. Clean out drawers, throw away gewgaws. Set pen to paper. Write—a letter, a poem, anything. Write.

Twelve-thirty P.M.

Luncheon. Friends. Salad, cold cuts. Wine. Gab away, talk drivel. Laugh. Observe the faces. Memorize the details of the faces. Hug the friends. Hug them deeply touched. But tearless. No tears at all.

Three-thirty P.M.

Phone Dr. Francisco. Ask if there's anything that can be done (quite unlikely); but say no to tranquilizers.

Six P.M.

Return home. Get the family together, including the baby of the family. Mention they'll be taken for a drive, and get the station wagon out of the garage. Head for the outskirts of the city. Find a spot on an elevation with a panoramic view. Park. Have everybody get out of the car. In a low, quiet voice, explain what is about to happen: the earth, which will open up (explain: as if it were parched), the bones, which will appear—the bones only, white, clean— bones that will then be covered with flesh, with hair, with eyes, with finger and toenails: men, women, laughing, crying.

Conclude with: It's about to begin, children. It's about to begin. Up to now, everything has been a lark.

EATING PAPER

I WORK FOR AN INSURANCE COMPANY. ONE DAY
the manager sends for me.

"I'd like you to meet Senhor Álvaro," he says,
introducing me to a thin young man with gloomy
eyes. "He's going to work for us and I'd like you to
show him the ropes."

Stealthily he thrusts a small piece of paper into my
pocket. While escorting Senhor Álvaro, I linger behind
him for a moment and read the note: "Watch out. He's
the Director's son." I wad the paper into a tiny ball
and swallow it nonchalantly. It hasn't been the first time.

I show our files to Senhor Álvaro.

"As you can see," I say to him, "we insure some
bigwigs."

He shows interest, writes down names.

I take him to my office, where a little fat man sits
waiting.

"I'd like to introduce you to a client who has come
to us to buy life insurance. . . ."

"Leave him to me." He addresses the man:

"Very well. So you would like to take out life
insurance. And when do you intend to die?"

"I . . ." mumbles the man, perplexed.

"You didn't understand my question," shouts Senhor Álvaro. "When do you intend to die?"

Startled, the man recoils in his chair. Senhor Álvaro turns to me:

"He doesn't know. They're a bunch of idiots, generally speaking. I'll try cause of death and see if it'll get me somewhere. So then, my friend, what are you planning to die of?"

The client gets up and makes a bolt for the door.

"Maybe that's not a very good technique," I suggest cautiously. I explain a few things about life insurance. A certain degree of optimism is necessary, I tell him. He heaves a sigh, seems to agree.

With satisfaction he informs the next client:

"There's no need to worry, my friend! Very few people have died recently."

The client looks at me and says he'll be back some other day.

I escort Senhor Álvaro back to the manager, and thrust a note into his pocket: "Impossible!" He swallows the paper with ease and leaves the room to get hold of the Director, who walks in with him shortly after. The Director asks us to leave him alone with Senhor Álvaro.

We pace back and forth in the corridor outside. From within come muffled outcries. Finally the door opens, Senhor Álvaro appears and looks straight at us with an ironic expression:

"So you think I'm not suitable. Very well. But you'll be hearing about my performance one of these days."

Lately, the Company has been on the brink of bankruptcy. Our most important clients have been dying mysteriously, one after the other. We've been swallowing notes from the Director without any letup. The manager is upset. As for myself, I think I have an idea as to the cause of these deaths.

THE EVIDENCE

BEFORE THE ACCIDENT I USED TO SELL VACUUM
cleaners and write poems. Sometimes I composed
verses during work hours. Once, as I was crossing
the street absentmindedly, I was run over by Senhor
Alexandre's luxury car.

One day when I have enough money
I'll win over the love of my sweet.
Then proudly I'll walk down the street
And—

And what? I don't know. I've forgotten. And
whose love did I want to win over? I don't know. All
I know is that I was well treated; my legs had to be
amputated, true, but Alexandre (out of guilt? out of
fear of being implicated?) took me in. There were
only the two of us and the servants in the big house.
We talked a great deal; the blithe, friendly kind of
conversation about trivialities. But invisible currents
of hatred, of repressed hostility would flow in the
moments of silence. For this reason we kept talking,
and we talked on and on. Until Alexandre suffered a

30

stroke that struck him dumb. It was sad. And now
here we are, the two of us, in Alexandre's bedroom,
facing each other in silence.

The doctor comes in. He's a bespectacled man,
melancholic but very efficient. He comes every day,
and even twice a day.

Medicine is dedication
with no breaks or vacation.

When Alexandre still spoke, he would insist that
the doctor examine me, too; and on such occasions he
would inquire about leg transplants, artificial limbs,
and so on. Alexandre was concerned. It's not his fault
that I am physically disabled. And thanks to him,
the doctor continues to follow up my case. However,
I do get short shrift.

"How are you doing? Fine? That's great, young
man. See you later."

His real concern is for Alexandre.

"Feeling any better, Senhor Alexandre?"

Alexandre does his best to answer; his face
becomes congested; the veins in his neck dilate. And
finally:

"Ga-ga-ga-ga . . ."

That's his answer. The doctor produces a smile.

"Very good, Senhor Alexandre! Your speech is
improving!"

The doctor examines him for a long time, then he
sighs. Alexandre's eyes meet mine. That's how we
carry on a conversation nowadays.

"Did you hear? He says I'm better," his eyes say.

"A lie," I reply. "He said that your speech has
improved. Which is not true either."

I'm angry because the physician didn't examine me
properly, he didn't even take my blood pressure.
However, I can now vent my anger on Alexandre,
even if it's only with my eyes. Misfortune has
equalized us.

We've done away with the oppressor,
now nobody feels oppressed,
now nobody feels abased,
now nobody feels insulted.

In comes blond Ester, Alexandre's niece.
"How is he, doctor?"
"So-so."
"Is he any better?"
"Neither better nor worse."
"And his heart?"
"So-so . . . He doesn't tolerate digitalis very
well. . . ."
Digitalis. Alexandre gets a shot of it for his heart.
At first they gave him pills, but he choked on them.
The doctor then prescribed injections. "Why don't
they grind the pills into powder? Why don't they
give him the medicine in liquid form?" I wondered. I
just wondered, without saying anything. After all,
the doctor knows best about Alexandre's heart.
    Blond Ester draws the doctor aside. We prick our
ears, Alexandre and I.
    "How much longer, doctor?" asks the niece in a
low voice, not too low, though; just low enough,
so that she sounds sad to the doctor, but not too low,
sure as she is that Alexandre can't hear, and whether
I can, well, she doesn't give a damn.
    "How long? . . ." The doctor sighs. "Who knows?
It could be a week. A month. A year . . ."
    Blond Ester's face looks afflicted.
    "Sometimes I think, doctor . . . All this struggle,
all this suffering. . . . Wouldn't it be better if we
stopped giving him medication so as to put an end to
this poor man's suffering?"
    Oh, no! I say to myself. And what about me,
what's going to happen to me then? You can barely
wait for the old man to die so that you can kick me
out! You're heartless! Let the old guy live! It might
be for just one week, but it might also be for another

month or year. Let nature run its course. Nature is
wise, it knows what it is doing. That's what I think.
But I don't voice my thoughts.

"Besides," the niece goes on, "what kind of life is
this? Can we call it life? There's more life in a head
of lettuce than in my uncle, doctor!"

"My young lady . . ." The doctor is ill at ease.

Ester leans toward the doctor. She has beautiful
breasts, I notice—I'm handicapped but not coma-
tose. The expression on her face changes, and so
does her voice, which is now full of tenderness.

"Think of the little children, doctor. Thousands of
starving little children everywhere. Have you thought
how many little children could be fed with the money
we've been spending to keep my uncle alive? A man
with a foot in the grave, a man whose heart no longer
tolerates digitalis?"

I look at Alexandre. I feel sorry for him. But I feel
sorry for the young woman, too. She sounds
sincere. And a poet can't help feeling touched before
such helpless altruism.

> *This beautiful young woman*
> *such pain she's been through:*
> *being unable to help the poor*
> *makes her feel oh-so-blue.*
> *And yet all that is needed*
> *for her dream to come true*
> *is rich uncle in a coffin*
> *if only this were true.*

The doctor takes his leave. The young woman
lingers for a while longer and then she too
leaves.

> *The young woman departs at last,*
> *night is falling fast,*
> *another day in the past.*

The following afternoon the doctor is examining
Alexandre. In comes Gregório, Alexandre's brother-in-
law and the manager of one of Alexandre's factories.

"How is he, doctor?"

"So-so."

"Is he any better?"

"Neither better nor worse."

"And his heart?"

"So-so . . . He doesn't tolerate digitalis very
well. . . ."

Gregório sits down. His hands are wringing his
gloves. He wants to ask something—this strong, tall
man with an anguished face. He hesitates; finally, he
gets up and draws the doctor aside.

"How much longer is this going to last, doctor?"

"Who knows? It could be a week. A month . . . A
year . . ."

"A year!"

Gregório is nervously striking the gloves against his
hand.

"A year!"

He walks up to the window and stands staring at
the cypresses in the garden. And it is from the
window that he says in a low, expressionless voice:

"I'm going to tell you something, doctor. I think
that very few people would be saddened by his
death."

"What are you saying?" The doctor is indignant.
"What about the family members? And the servants,
to whom he has been a veritable father?"

"A father!" Gregório laughs with bitterness. "You
have no idea, sir! A cruel man, that's what he is. He
made them work for peanuts, he was always abusing
everybody in sight, and punishing people left and
right!"

Alexandre doesn't even blink. It's my eyes that
brim with tears. My heart is anguished. I can't bear
to watch this scene.

This scene is unbearable
tears roll down my face
when I see such a disgrace
—the powerful man treated like a dog!

The doctor doesn't say a word. Gregório takes his leave.

Gregório departs at last,
night is falling fast,
another day in the past.

The following afternoon the doctor is examining Alexandre when Maria, the patient's sister, comes in. And how is he, doctor, so-so, is he any better, neither better nor worse, and his heart, and so on and so forth—she draws the doctor aside and goes straight to the point:

"If we were to get the inheritance now, doctor . . . I have a son who's about to enter the university. . . ."

Just then, in walks an attractive young man; he greets the doctor, is apprised of the matter under discussion, and corroborates his mother's words:

"My mother is right, doctor. My greatest dream is to attend the school of medicine. But it's going to be difficult. . . . My father is dead. . . . I need money to pay for the college preparatory course, to buy books. Doctor, help me! You're the model I want to emulate. Show your solidarity to a future colleague!"

The doctor, horrified:

"Vultures! Get out!"

Vultures, get out,
shouted the doctor,
it's time no doubt
for some compassion.

All three have left. Alexandre and I look at each other.

"I can't believe it," he says with his eyes.

"Well, Alexandre. They're upset. But deep in their hearts they want your welfare."

"Do they?"

"Sure, you'll see."

A nurse comes in (there are two of them, the day and the night nurse) and begins to prepare an injection of digitalis. The door opens and in comes Ester, her eyes brimming with tears.

"Dear uncle, I'm so sorry! Is there anything I can do for you?"

"Excuse me," says the nurse, holding the hypodermic.

"Leave it to me, nurse," shouts Ester. "Leave it to me, I'll give my uncle the injection."

"This is my job," says the woman dryly. "Will you please get out of my way."

Ester snatches the hypodermic away.

"You stupid woman! Witch! No wonder my uncle is so ill, looked after by viragos like you. Get out, now!"

Offended, the nurse walks away. Ester gives her uncle a shot, tucks him in, and kisses him good-bye on the forehead.

Soon afterward, Gregório comes in.

"I'm so sorry!"

He's both sorry and outraged. He has run into the nurse at the gate. "There's no way I'll ever give that old man another injection, I won't lift a finger anymore," the woman had allegedly said. Gregório was indignant.

"The idiot! She didn't look after you! But from now on things will be different. I'll personally take care of everything. Including the injections!"

He takes a sterilized hypodermic and prepares an injection of digitalis.

"Ga-ga-ga-ga . . ." Alexandre, terrified, attempts to extricate his arm.

"He would rather have the shot in his buttocks,"

says Gregório, commiserating with him. "Poor man! His arms must be quite sore after the shots given by that virago."

"It's that . . ." I say timidly.

"Shut up, parasite!" yells Gregório. "I'll reckon with you later."

If he wants me to shut up, then I shut up. In silence I watch Gregório give Alexandre a shot of digitalis, after which he leaves. Still in silence, I watch Maria come in. She lives nearby.

"From my window I saw the nurse bolting. What a hussy!"

She gives him another injection and leaves. Soon after in comes the future doctor, who has been making passes at the nurse, an activity related to his interest in medicine.

"Dear Uncle, I've heard that the nurse didn't give you an injection and that she won't be working here anymore. Don't worry. She was incompetent. Besides, she was frigid, too. So, I'll be looking after you. As you'll see, I'm already experienced."

He is. It takes him one minute to give his uncle an injection of digitalis and leave the room. The night nurse arrives, looks at the notes written by her colleague:

"That tart didn't give him an injection!"

Alexandre no longer offered any resistance.

As for myself, I've always been a man of few words; I'd much rather write poems. But out of consideration for the old man, I said something to the nurse. It's cold here, that's what I mumbled, but she didn't hear me, or if she did, she chose to ignore me. Too bad.

It's cold in here.
Alexandre will die.
Both the hill and the river weep
as they watch a man die.

There was no ministration
of either liquid or powder medication.
And they wouldn't listen to
anything I said.
Thus, Alexandre dies
from too many injections.
He'll live on in my recollections
and in our big heart, too.

THE OFFERINGS OF THE
DALILA STORE

EVERYTHING IS FINE IN SÃO PAULO, I'M HAPPY
with my job managing a store chain—a good house,
two cars, a trip to the Caribbean already booked,
everything—when all of a sudden I get a phone call
from my mother in Porto Alegre. My old man is
sick, she finds herself unable to cope with looking
after the house and running their business.

I'm an only son. I fly out on the first flight
available.

I find my father much better. However, since I'm
here, I decide I might as well straighten out their
business affairs; they own a small men's clothing store
in Mont'Serrat. They could make ends meet when it
was the only such store in the area, patronized by a
loyal clientele consisting mostly of civil servants and
small businessmen. Thanks to the store, I was able to
go to college and graduate. That's the reason why
nowadays my diploma in accounting hangs behind the
cash register, together with the business license and
the picture of my grandfather, the founder of this
commercial establishment.

Now, however, I see that there's another store on

this street, right across from ours—the Dalila Store.
Small and untidy like ours, and yet business is much
livelier there. Why? I wonder, looking at the owner,
an old woman with bleached hair and painted eyes
who stares at me defiantly from her door. She has
no idea whom she is up against.

I get to work on this problem. A preliminary
investigation reveals the fact that a substantial number of our customers now patronize the Dalila Store.
And I soon find out why: the receipts issued by the
store entitle the customers to attend certain movie
sessions held in the back of the Dalila Store on
Friday nights. I get hold of some of these receipts.
And I book a seat on a plane flying out on
Saturday. I intend to solve this matter in my own
way: quickly, efficiently, quietly.

Wearing dark glasses and a false mustache, I ring
the doorbell at the Dalila Store at 9 P.M. on Friday.
The door opens; the painted face of the old woman
appears. I produce my proof of purchase, step in,
and am taken to a poorly lit room in the back of the
store. There, amid the smiling mannequins and
boxes of merchandise, I find the other members of the
audience. As it turns out, I'm not the only one
wearing dark glasses. I sit down on a rustic wooden
bench, light a cigarette, and wait.

Dona Dalila is nervous. She runs about the room,
straightens the torn screen, looks at her watch;
finally she announces in a hoarse voice that the movie
is about to start. She switches off the light and turns
on the old, noisy movie projector.

A caption appears on the screen: THE ADVEN-
TURES OF DALILA. Even before the movie starts I
guess what it is: one of those wretched pornographic
movies, old, dark, silent—the woman with the dog,
the woman with two men, the woman with another
woman. And indeed, the first scene already depicts a
bed; and from amid the furs and the feathers emerges
the face of the debauchee: eyes painted black,

heart-shaped mouth—beautiful, this slut, despite
everything.

In comes the dog; then the two men; then another
woman. The audience laughs and applauds; some
even moan with excitement.

The movie is over. The light is turned on. Mutter-
ings; somebody wants more. No, says the old
woman, that's all for today. There's more next
Friday. And don't forget to bring your receipts.

Half-hidden behind a mannequin, I wait until
everybody is gone. The old woman is rewinding the
film. I leave my hiding place; she's startled to see me.

"What is it?" she yells, enraged. "It's over! Scram!
Out with you, it's late and I still have lots to do."

I remove the mustache and the glasses. Surprised,
she steps back: "But it's Dona Cecilia's son!"

"That's right," I say, adding: "the son of your
competitors. I am here to put an end to this circus."

Incredulous, she laughs. "Put an end, how? Why?"

"Because it's an unfair competition," I say. "That's
the only reason."

"Your parents can do the same in their store," she
remarks with sarcasm.

"Shut up!" I yell (but mine is a calculated fury).
"My parents are not trash like you, you bitch.
They're honest people."

She is frightened. "There's no need to shout, I'm
not deaf; besides, what's wrong with showing a
few movies?"

"It's a dirty trick," I shout, "to attract customers
by such means."

She sighs. "All right," she says. "I won't show
movies anymore." She begins to remove the film
reel from the projector.

"Give it to me," I tell her.

"What for?" Her voice is tremulous, and there's
genuine terror in her eyes. Ah!

"Give it to me!" I say again.

She tries to escape through the back door. I grab

her and snatch the reel away. She tries to fight back. I placate her with a good punch.

"I'm going to burn this filth," I say, still puffing. "Right here and right now."

"Wait a moment!" The tone of voice is entreating and her mouth is bleeding. "Do me just one favor, will you? Let me watch this movie for one last time."

"Why?"

"Let me show the movie, will you? Then I'll explain."

I look at my watch. I still have time; besides, I didn't see the movie right.

"Okay."

She puts the reel in the projector, turns off the light. I sit down on the bench and light a cigarette. She sits down next to me. We look at the face on the screen—at the painted eyes, at the heart-shaped mouth.

"Do you know who she is?" she murmurs in my ear. "That's me."

"You're lying."

"I'm not, honest. That's me, in Europe. I was very famous. . . . The beautiful Dalila."

I look at her. Indeed, I seem to recognize in her fat face the features of the woman on the screen.

"Let's look at the movie again."

There's no doubt about it: the same eyes, the same mouth.

"That's me all right," she whispers, and laughs.

We sank to the floor, amid the mannequins.

On Saturday morning I'm in an airplane heading for São Paulo. I've already persuaded my parents to sell their store to Dalila; I've already arranged for a monthly allowance, which I'll send them from São Paulo; and I've already made up my mind that I won't be returning to the Mont'Serrat district in Porto Alegre in the foreseeable future.

THE SHORT-STORY WRITERS

EVERYBODY WENT TO RAMIRO'S AFTERNOON OF
autographs. Every single one of the forty or fifty
short-story writers. I was one of the first to arrive: I
didn't want to miss the hot dogs. I was out of luck: I
was only the tenth person to have arrived there but
all I could see was half a sausage and adulterated
whiskey. Which didn't prevent me from hugging
Ramiro effusively. What's the matter, man, he asked,
and I said, Nothing, there's nothing the matter,
Ramiro, nothing, really. And I added: Congratula-
tions on your book, Ramiro, I haven't gotten
around to reading it yet but I understand it's very
good; as a matter of fact, I've always thought of
you as a guy who has made it. One of the very few.
(I was getting maudlin, an afternoon of autographs
affects me in this way.) Thank you, said Ramiro, we
try to do what we can. What about you, he asked,
what have you been up to? Nothing, I said, except
working my ass off at the newspaper, that's all.

"Writing anything?"

Yes, indeed, I was. I was writing a short story
called "The Short-Story Writers."

Ramiro laughed and excused himself; he had to autograph a book for an elderly aunt of his who lived in a rest home and had come especially for the occasion.

There was no sign of hot dogs but more people were coming. Orlando approached me; he was about to ask me to lend him money; by the look on my face he saw it would be no use. So he asked me what I was writing. A short story called "The Short-Story Writers," I replied. That's the way, man, let 'em have it, the short story in the state of Santa Catarina has been waiting for someone to rejuvenate it. I'm not from Santa Catarina, I said, but he had already moved on. Poor Orlando, always in such a muddle.

I've heard he has cancer, whispered Marisa. And what's worse, she went on, he doesn't seek treatment, he can't afford to go to the hospital, he doesn't contribute toward the social security. Besides, she concluded, he's a jerk. I agreed, watching the back door, through which, for some reason, I expected a man to come in with hot dogs.

And what about you, asked Marisa, what are you writing? A short story called "The Short-Story Writers," I said. You're a jerk too, Marisa was laughing. She never missed an afternoon of autographs, not Marisa, and she was always laughing. I was laughing, too: That's right, Marisa, I'm a jerk. She laughed and laughed; she was looking at me and I was looking at her, thinking what a knockout she was. One of these days I'll have to talk with her; not now, though, now I'm dying for a hot dog. And a drink.

Standing beside me, short-story writer Nathan was saying that we short-story writers moan and grind our teeth as we produce our short stories. Meanwhile, the short-story writer went on, we ignore the radio programs, the television soap operas, the gossip columns in the newspapers, the Technicolor movies,

the weekly magazines, the politicians, the civil servants, the gossip column writers, the new rich, the
bourgeoisie, the demagogues, the socially committed
writers, the platitudes, the sonnets, such words as
despair, tenderness, fate, twilight, heart, soul. . . . And
painstakingly, Nathan went on, we plod away at
our short stories. Our characters are nameless; they
are just he. "He lit a cigarette and lay staring at the
ceiling." The sharpest among our readers, remarked
Nathan, realize that we are referring to ourselves;
that we are engaging ourselves in a dialogue with our
own personal demons; that from the bottom of our
souls we are pouring out a clear, lukewarm liquid that
turns cold and turbid when exposed to the raw light
of the world, and what's more: This liquid solidifies
and is turned into a hard gemstone whose nature is
unknown but whose value can only be appreciated by
a few rare connoisseurs, really admirable creatures.
A gemstone resembling opal. While we wait for
recognition, continued Nathan, who was waxing
excited, we lie on our dirty beds, we light up ciga-
rettes and stare at the ceiling. We suffer the pangs
imposed by a dull, amorphous world. We think we
could swallow this world as if it were a tiny pill.
Why don't we? Is it out of pity—or is it out of fear
that we might find out that this particle is indeed
larger than our gullets? Idiots, shouted Nathan, we're
such idiots! Let's admit it! Like everybody else, we
eat, we fuck, we breathe—but we are half dead, we're
zombies. We only begin to live—and at this point
Nathan was really bellowing—when we painfully give
birth to our sad sentences, which lie forgotten on
bookshelves, pages and pages, letter after letter—but
these letters don't touch each other, waiting as they
are for the intellectual adventurer, for the consumer,
an entity entirely dependent upon the laws of the
marketplace. Supply and demand! concluded short-
story writer Nathan.

   After listening to this rant of his, I sneaked away. I

joined a group: Milton, Capaverde, and Afonso. A photographer came up to us and took a picture. Then he wanted to charge us for it. I got raving mad; I had thought he was someone from my newspaper. I'm not paying you anything, I yelled, I should be charging you instead for having posed. The photographer swore at us and left the bookstore. Good riddance, I bellowed after him.

Ramiro was busy autographing books for this one here, for that one there. Poy was watching and saying to me: This book of his is not going to sell, it's much too entangled, much too hermetic. People want simple stuff, bread and cheese kind of thing. This reminded me of the hot dogs and I glanced around: plenty of short-story writers but no food in sight.

"And what about you," asked Poy, "what are you writing?"

A short story called "The Short-Story Writers," I replied. It's hopeless, Poy assured me, we should be writing for radio, for television. Books are expensive, books are difficult, there's no future in books, it's even worse with fiction. I've given up on books, Poy was saying; I'm trying to get into a different line of work, I have this brother-in-law who works for television, he'll see if he can land me a job. My eyes were searching for Marisa, or hot dogs, but all I could see was short-story writers.

"Some short-story writers," it was Nathan speaking again, "refuse to take part in any kind of activity. They don't eat, they don't drink, they hardly write. They're bogged down by apathy, waiting for someone to tell them: Wake up, lucid prophets!"

I caught sight of short-story writer Lúcio, who wrote only after going through a meticulous ritual: he closed the windows, lit candles, put on a tuxedo, then sat down at a jacaranda table made in Bahia. I caught sight of short-story writer Armando, who always wrote with a fountain pen. I caught sight of

short-story writer Celomar, who went to the seaside
to write; and of short-story writer Guerra, who
went to the mountains. I caught sight of short-story
writer Jerônimo, who wrote first the end, then the
beginning, then the middle.

I caught sight of short-story writer Volmir. Whenever short-story writer Volmir wanted to write, he
would closet himself in his study for two or more
days. When he reappeared, he was changed but
happy. He would invite his wife and daughters into
his study, where they would stand around the desk
upon which lay the typed pages held together with a
brand-new paper clip. Full of jubilant respect, they
would stare at the short story for several minutes.
"What's the title?" the wife would ask, and when
the short-story writer disclosed it, they would hug
one another, overcome by joy.

Short-story writer Murtinho organized the production of his short stories in accordance with the
assembly-line principles: outlines in the top drawer,
half-finished short stories in the second drawer,
finished short stories in the third drawer.

Short-story writer Manduca, quite soused, hugs me
whimpering:

"I can only write under the influence of bennies and
lately they haven't had any effect. . . . I've been
taking the weirdest things, I've even tried deodor-
ant. . . ."

"I'm writing a short story called 'The Short-Story
Writers.' I'll keep in mind what you've told me."

I don't remember exactly when I began to write. It
must have been something that sneaked up on me.
When I became aware, I was already working with
paper and pencil. I would watch people, animals,
and things, and would imagine how they would look
under the form of words. And so I began to shape
my sentences, at first with great difficulty; after a

period of time, all I had to do was to let my hand
slide across the sheet of paper and observe how the
words looked on the page; at the dawn of my life I
would appraise my own work by taking into account
the length of the sentences, the slant of each letter,
the number of smears on the page: when a short story
was good, it also looked neat. I would hold it at a
distance, admire it for a while—and it was time for
me to write another short story. Rain or shine, sleet
or fog—there I was, keeping at it!

Short-story writer Katz selected ten famous short-
story writers. From each one he picked five short
stories at random. He found out the average number
of words in each sentence, the words most fre-
quently used, and other such parameters. With the
data collected, he composed a short story—which he
considered perfect. Not everybody shared his opinion.

Short-story writer Almeirindo insisted that his book
be printed in lower-case letters only and in very fine
print. It's going to be rather hard to read, warned the
owner of the print shop. It doesn't matter, said
short-story writer Almeirindo, I'm paying, I can have
the book printed any way I want. In sharp contrast
with him, short-story writer Cabrão had written an
entire chapter in which each word took up a full
page.

Short-story writer Almir misplaced the last page of
his short story "The Glory." He spent two days
rummaging the house in search of it. Suddenly
realizing that the short story was really much better
just the way it was, he gave up the search.

I've once written a short story in two minutes, but
on another occasion it took me six months to write
one. In one single drawer I counted twenty-seven
short stories; under my bed I found a briefcase with
sixteen short stories, whose existence I had entirely
forgotten. At that time I had been writing a short

story called "The Short-Story Writers" and I had been looking for a young woman called Marisa, or was it a drink? The whiskey turned up first, brought in by a sullen-looking waiter.

The dream of short-story writer Reinaldo was a short story that would write itself: given the theme, or the first word at the most—all the other words would inevitably follow. The short-story writer visualized a pen set to paper, wires connected to a machine, some feedback gadget to correct possible stylistic or other deviations. Short-story writer Damasceno had in mind a multiple-choice kind of short story, written in the second-person singular: "It was a summer afternoon. You were: a) home; b) at the movies; c) in a bookstore. If (a) is true . . ." Short-story writer Auro was thinking of impregnating the pages of his books with hallucinogenic substances. By licking the paper, the reader would have erratic visions.

I caught sight of Marisa. She was sitting in her car in front of the bookstore. The car door was open, exposing her legs. Hell, how can anyone be such a knockout, I groaned. I really needed a car. If I had a car, Marisa would now be sitting next to me, with my hand constantly sliding down the gear-shift onto her thigh. But I didn't have a car; on foot I moved among the short-story writers.

Short-story writers. Their origin is lost in the darkness of time.

"Waiter!" I called out, rather loudly. The short-story writers turn around to stare. "Waiter!" I say again, lowering my voice. "Whiskey, waiter!"

There is some information available on a mysterious tribe of storytellers in Central Asia, who used to roam from region to region to tell their stories. Nobody knows anything concrete about those mysterious storytellers, who allegedly were decimated by hostile peoples. . . . Masterpieces of the short story can be found in the Bible. . . . The Persian storytell-

ers believed that certain seeds sown on a night of
full moon would bring forth trees that yielded hollow
fruit, inside which were very brief short stories with
one, or at the most, two characters each. . . . Story-
teller Scheherazade told the sultan more than a
thousand stories, thereby ensuring her survival. In his
first book, short-story writer Hebel depicted Nazi
Germany accurately; and he did it again in his second
and third book. Uneasy, people would wonder:
When will he stop depicting Nazi Germany so
accurately?

Short-story writers are ubiquitous. In the book *The
Family of Man* there is a photograph taken by Nat
Farbman (*Life*) in what was formerly Bechuanaland; it
shows an African narrating something to his fellow
Africans. There is no explanatory caption, but one can
be sure that the man is telling a story; and his
audience, albeit small, is attentive.

In the Middle Ages some storytellers accused of
witchcraft were burned alive. In certain regions of
Italy, their ashes are kept in small bottles; shortly
before exam time, students go on a pilgrimage to
such regions to venerate the remains of those
storytellers.

What is a short story? People have been arguing
about it. Let's rephrase the question more appropri-
ately: What characterizes the short story? For short-
story-writer Poe—Poe, hm!—brevity, a demand of
modern life. I agree, says short-story writer Jones,
adding: Let's not forget the role of the subway,
which demands stories short enough for commuters
to read at one sitting. According to Jones, the
concept of teamwork—an outcome of the Industrial
Revolution—fostered the appearance of short-story
anthologies.

The short story reached its peak during the nineteenth
century (with Poe, Chekhov, Maupassant). Nowadays it doesn't enjoy the same prestige it once had,
according to short-story writer Eulálio. Short-story

writer Poy blames television for the decline of the
short story, whereas short-story writer Tomás thinks
that the cause of the decline lies in the disappearance
of the wood-burning stove, around which the
family used to gather to listen to short stories being
read aloud.

I think that from the beginning I enjoyed listening
to stories. Sitting on the curb of the sidewalk, I'd
listen to the other kids that lived on my street tell
about the woman who had decapitated her husband,
about the airplane pilot who had shot down twelve
enemy planes, about the movie that they had
watched on Sunday. As a matter of fact, I too had
gone to the movie theater, where amid the deafen-
ing screams of the audience I had looked at the figures
moving on the screen. . . . And yet, it was only
after listening to my friends tell the story line of the
movie that everything became clear to me; the
action made sense, the climax was revealed through
the appropriate tone of voice of the narrator; and
only then would I feel the authentic emotion that had
eluded me in the movie theater although I had paid
for my admission ticket.

My friends had a knack for telling a story. Today
they are businessmen or professionals in various
fields. . . . Not one of them is a writer. I think that
the idea of writing simply never occurred to them.
If only they had tried, if only they had scribbled just a
few words. . . . In the end, I was the one who
decided to get entangled with words & lies.

Young short-story writer Afonso is now approach-
ing. A chubby fellow, he minces up to me and gives
me a short story to read. It's called "The Eye Within
the Eye." Interesting. Afonso skillfully depicts the
life of Hermes, a loner who works for a big company. We follow Hermes from the moment when
he wakes up in a modest house in the suburbs; we see
him making coffee according to a routine established
years before (Hermes is in his forties, Afonso informs

me); we see him on the bus on his way to work; later we see him sitting at his desk, typing away the company letters. He eats lunch—by himself—in a cafeteria and returns to the office, picking his teeth with a toothpick.

Afonso writes well and he started just a short while ago.

But back to the story: After leaving the office at the end of the day, Hermes strolls about the city center, looks into the store windows, and ogles at the women. Sometimes he returns home with someone he picked up, says Afonso; more often, however, he buries himself in a movie theater. He rather enjoys comedies.

Sitting in the nearly empty theater, indifferent to the fleas, Hermes gets all worked up over the movie: he laughs, talks to himself:

"Look at Fatso! Such a numbskull, this roly-poly fool! Hey, Fatso!"

At this point Afonso turns the lights on. We see Hermes blushing as he casts glances around him. We see him leave slowly, his head lowered. What is he going to do next? Some foolishness?

No: Afonso has him in the men's room. There he stays while the minutes trickle away. The next movie has just begun and—look! Hermes is leaving the men's room. He looks around for a good seat, sits down and:

"Hey, look at Fatso!"

Short-story writer Levino leaves the theater deeply impressed by the movie about a short-story writer. He is going to do exactly what the leading character in the movie did. He strides back and forth in his bedroom, his lips compressed, his eyes fixed upon the floor; suddenly, he sits down at the typewriter, inserts a sheet of paper and, just like the short-story writer in the movie, takes a deep breath, then starts typing at a fast pace, keeping at it for a full five minutes; he lights up a cigarette, takes a long pull at it, holds the sheet of paper up by the upper left-hand corner, reads what he has written so far; he types away for another five minutes, reads again. Just like the short-story writer in the movie, he rips the paper off the typewriter, crumples the paper up and angrily tosses it into the wastebasket. As in the movie, it was a crummy short story.

Short-story writer Guilherme, a former seminarian, arrives.

"Am I late?"

"I'm afraid so," I say, already slurring my words.

"Too bad. I've almost finished my book of short stories, I don't have time for anything else. What have you been doing?"

"Writing a short story called 'The Short-Story Writers.' "

"Are you going to portray us?"

I write. The writer writes. He has to cover page after page with writing.

At first I only aspired to do what my friends did with such liveliness as they sat on the curb of the sidewalk: to tell a story. However, the truth of the matter is that I became fascinated by the possibility of reducing my friend Lelo, today an engineer, to "a diminutive fellow." Poor Lelo: there he was, all of a sudden, motionless, frozen, reduced to a miniature. Headhunters must experience some such similar sensation. Still not satisfied, I then compared his nose with a parrot's beak. Actually, years later he came down with a disease called psittacosis, which is apparently transmitted by parrots. The curse of the short-story writer?

It could be. Hatred inspired short-story writer José Homero; after being evicted from his apartment, he wrote a bitter short-story about tenancy. The landlord oppresses the tenant, takes away his money, his furniture, his wife. The oppressed tenant ends up machine-gunning the oppressor. A poignant sentence describes the lease agreement lying on the floor, spattered with blood. At the end of the story, the tenant opens the window and sees the rising sun heralding a new day. To satirize his enemies, short-story writer Catarino depicted them as animals. When he ran out of well-known animals, he resorted to the exotic fauna—the ornithorhynchus, the koala; to prehistoric creatures—the brontosaur, the dinosaur; and to mythological animals—the unicorn. In an index as thick as a phone book he listed the names of his enemies and their corresponding animals.

Back in my hometown I once had a short story of mine called "A Family of the Interior" published in the Sunday supplement of a newspaper. Very well. On Monday night I was alone at home, peacefully reading a short story when there was a knock on the door. As soon as I opened it I was greeted with a violent shove that sent me rolling on the floor. When I got to my feet, I was face to face with my neighbor, Senhor Antonio. A big mustachioed man— well, nothing wrong with that—but he was holding a gun and it was loaded.

"Very well, you son of a bitch," he said, "I know that your parents aren't home, so the two of us can have a nice quiet chat. Be very careful about what you're going to say because your life will depend on this conversation of ours."

"What have I done, Senhor Antonio?" I stuttered.

"What have you done?" he shouted. The man sounded really mad. "What have you done? So, you don't know? What about this here?"

He took a newspaper clipping out of his pocket. It was my short story.

"What do you take me for? An idiot? Do you think

that I don't know who you are referring to? 'A fat man,' you say here. Who is this fat man? Who else in this neighborhood weighs over one hundred kilograms? 'The fat man owned a bar,' you wrote. It so happens that I'm fat and that I own a grocery store. Bar, grocery store—pretty similar, wouldn't you say?"

He pressed the gun against my chest. Even in this dire predicament of mine, the writer in me showed through! "His beady, bloodshot eyes were filled with rage," I observed.

"You're rather smart, kid. But not as smart as you may think. You want to describe my life as being a dull routine: 'Every day after dinner, they would sit down and listen to the radio. . . .'" Now, listening to the radio might be dull to you. But is it for everybody else? Can you imagine what a joy it is when we succeed in turning in to a foreign radio station? 'On Sundays they ate chicken.' So what? Are all chickens alike? Are all Sundays alike?"

He stopped, took a deep breath.

"But worst of all," he went on in a strangled voice, "is the way you end the short story, saying that I kill my wife, that I dissolve her body in acid so as to leave no traces. . . . What do you mean? Acid doesn't leave any traces?"

At that moment we heard noises at the front door. Senhor Antonio, fat but nimble, fled through the back door and I ran to my bedroom. Quickly I jotted down what I had seen in the man's eyes: "Genuine interest, anxious expectancy . . ."

Antonio died before his wife: He suffered an infarct when he caught his wife in bed with a neighbor (it wasn't me, some other neighbor). "I was up to here with that routine," she said at the funeral.

It wasn't always, however, that my short stories had this kind of outcome. For instance, I never succeeded in upsetting alderman Ximenes, a venal politician whom I particularly abhorred. I satirized him by depicting him as the rotten apple that clings to the branch even after the death of the apple tree ("Autumn Is Over"); as the tick that poisons his fellow ticks with DDT so that he can have the bull all for himself ("One for All"); as the king who steals his own crown and then accuses his enemies ("To Arms, Citizens!"). My friends would praise these stories, although admitting that they couldn't make head or tail of them. As for the alderman, he was my greatest admirer. At a city council meeting he made a motion that a literary prize be established as an incentive to the city's short-story writers; he told me confidentially that he had me in mind when he wrote the draft bill: "I'm sure you'll win the prize. And if I can use my clout with the selection committee, you've got the prize in the bag. No need to thank me, I like people with a flair for writing, with a talent for literature." He himself was a short-story writer of sorts, who wrote but sporadically.

In order to castigate the likes of him I needed power. I had it and wielded it, I can assure you. Autumn would come and go, I would write and presto! three months were thus subtracted from the life of a protagonist. In my short stories the protagonist went from the cradle to the grave hopping like a grasshopper on the sand, leaving his faint imprints upon it.

Gradually I became less and less interested in the hopping itself and began to focus my attention on the imprints, which I would describe to the best of my abilities. Finally I set the imprints aside, too, and was left only with the words: I no longer concerned myself with the characters and their stories. Of course, my short stories became unintelligible. What did I care? Let the readers brace themselves for the crossing of this region of dense bushes and quicksands. Great discoveries would lie in store for those brave enough to set out on this intellectual adventure. The small number of my readers didn't

surprise me: many are called, few are chosen, was my
belief.

Suddenly I was assailed by doubts. I began to
mistrust the demons inside me, the demons that
kept manufacturing and sending to the surface sentences that I was to imprint on paper. Did they really
know what they were talking about? And if they
didn't, what was to be done with the growing stack
of short stories? I took to drinking.

Which merely worsened matters because during my
lucid moments my fate became crystal clear. Nobody would ever read my work. The thousands of
kindred spirits who supposedly would flock into my
bedroom demanding short stories would never mate-
rialize. And I was more lonely than ever. Not even
the passionate glances of Senhor Antonio's widow
were enough to comfort me. That is what the crisis
in the life of the short-story writer is like, a terrible
episode.

Short-story writer César, while rereading his first
short stories, exclaimed:

"But I was a much better writer then!"

Afterward he went years without writing.

"What wouldn't I give to be able to experience
anti-gravity," short-story writer W., who wrote
science fiction, would say with longing. "Me? I don't
talk to anybody. If anybody wants to find out about
me, they should read my short stories," stated short-
story writer Ordovaz, who lived in a cottage in the
suburbs and subsisted on lettuce and canned food.

I was born in a small town in the interior. I've
been writing ever since I was a child. My first short
story was called "The Notary Public's Wife." At the
age of nineteen, I came to the big city, bringing with
me a suit, two shirts, and a blue briefcase with
many short stories. None of these short stories ever
got published but I succeeded in getting a job

working for a newspaper. And I met many short-story writers: I met them at social gatherings, at birthday parties, in movie theaters, at university student organizations. "We sprout like mushrooms!" said short-story writer Michel.

"I'll kill myself if my book isn't sold out!" said short-story writer Osmar. "A warning to the public." When the book didn't sell out, short-story writer Osmar shot himself in the chest. He was seriously but not fatally wounded; he was left with an ugly scar. On the beach, short-story writer Osmar had to wear a T-shirt.

Short-story writer Odair wrote quietly for twelve years. Nothing he wrote ever got published. He kept his work in big manila envelopes and never mentioned his writing to anyone. One day he looked at the stack of envelopes—eighty centimeters high—and despairing, he cried out:

"What's the use?"

He threw the short stories into the fire. Changing his mind before it was too late, he took them out of the flames, burning himself a little. However, some of his best short stories—"Despair," for instance—were lost forever. Others were severely damaged.

After returning home drunk from an evening of autographs, I threw seventy-three short stories up into the air; the pages were scattered throughout my bedroom. On the following day, the owner of the boarding house where I lived threw away the mass of paper, which was soiled with vomit. When I woke up, I ran to the garbage can, but it was too late; the garbage truck had already been there. I found the beginning of a short story lying in the gutter. It described some very personal suffering. I left it right there, hoping that a curious passerby would read it.

Short-story writer Otaviano wrote his short stories in public toilets, where they appeared in the form of graffiti on the walls. Whenever he was in the middle of a short story, someone would invariably start knocking on the door, asking him to hurry up; short-story writer Otaviano was then forced to finish the story in another stall. Fragments of his short stories are to be found scattered throughout the public toilets of the city.

Short-story writer Pascoal threw a party at his house; he invited his friends, secretly taped their conversations, then used actual quotes to write a short story. He showed it to his friends, who weren't amused.

"What's the world coming to," wondered Pascoal, anguished, "when people don't like what they say?"

After a while I was overcome by the urge to write again. My job at the newspaper was exhausting, but even so I still had time left for literature. What I lacked were certain conditions, such as the right props. For instance, I didn't have a good typewriter. Without further delay, I bought an electric one, which was perfect; however, it didn't work when there was a power failure—at the very moment when I was hit by inspiration. I also bought a desk, a swivel armchair, a pair of lined slippers. In addition, with the intention of promoting my short stories, I began to coordinate my public relations activities: I got a good supply of liquor, I made off with the address book of a literary critic, I cultivated the friendship of a gossip columnist, etc.

Such things took up a lot of my time, and what's worse, they cost me a bundle. The salary from the newspaper was no longer enough. I had to moonlight as an instructor in a typing course (I had to lend them my own typewriter); I was now working day and night. That's all right, I would say to myself, it's only until I can lay the groundwork for my literary production; afterward, I'll have plenty of time for writing. But I got tired of waiting. Then in one single night I quit my evening job, threw away

the address book, and quarreled with the gossip
columnist.

Problems. Short-story writer Caio can produce one
short story every two hours. Knowing that 50
percent of these short stories are bad, 25 percent
are so-so, and 25 percent are good, how many
short stories can short-story writer Caio produce in
one day, and how many of them will be good, how
many so-so, and how many bad? Answer: Short-story
writer Caio can produce twelve short stories per
day, six of which are bad, three so-so, and three
(hurray!) good.

But things don't work out in such a mathematical
way with short-story writer Caio. . . . He needs
eight hours of sleep per day. He has tried to get by
with less sleep, but he can't: he becomes irritable
and gets a headache. Therefore, he is left with sixteen
hours, during which the short-story writer could
write eight short stories, four of which would be bad,
two so-so, and two good.

However, short-story writer Caio has to *eat* as well.
He has already tried to live on nothing but sand-
wiches so that he wouldn't waste time with regular
meals, but he lost weight, became undernourished,
and even lost interest in writing. Nowadays he is
more careful and sets aside two hours for meals,
knowing that he still has another fourteen hours,
during which he could write seven short stories,
three and a half of which would be bad, one and three
quarters good, and one and three quarters so-so
(luckily, short-story writer Caio knows his fractions
well, common or otherwise).

But . . . short-story writer Caio has to earn a living,
too. He has already tried to live off literature but
found it impossible. The best he could do was to get
a job working six hours a day, which left him an
additional eight hours, during which he could write
four short stories: two bad, one so-so, one good.

Furthermore, he has to read: books, newspapers,

magazines. Otherwise he wouldn't be up-to-date, would lose contact with the world, and would deprive himself of the influence of various other writers (some good, some so-so, some bad—yet, one should experience everything). And then there is television, too—not all programs are good, but at least the *medium* deserves scrutiny; and there are movies, plays, concerts; and jazz records—a foible of the short-story writer, an indulgence without which he would run the risk of becoming narrow-minded. Such activities take up two hours on the average; the remaining six hours could be the equivalent of three bad short stories, one-and-a-half so-so short stories, and one-and-a-half good short stories.

Short-story writer Caio has a family. Wife and two kids, a normal family. Naturally, the short-story writer plays with his children—and tells them stories (which he could count as part of his output but doesn't because they are not properly recorded—unless one were to consider the children's unconscious a book, as some people claim it is. The short-story writer would rather not count on this possibility).

As for his wife, she's beautiful. . . . Well-versed in the art of seductive smiles to lure the short-story writer. He gives in and is rewarded with immense pleasure. Sometimes he feels guilty and thinks that only priests have the ideal conditions to become short-story writers. But he can't ignore the urges of his own body; besides, how could he describe love scenes if he didn't make love?

Consequently, the short-story writer devotes half an hour a day to his wife. There's this, that, and the other, a caress and other things like that. . . . The short-story writer is a refined, sensitive man. Could a short-story writer be otherwise?

Well then. Such activities with the family take up two hours a day; there are four hours left, which means two short stories, one bad and one half-so-so, half-good.

There are also other things that eat into whatever time is left. The short-story writer suffers from constipation and spends half an hour a day in the bathroom. He has already tried to write there, but without success; it seems that the two activities are mutually exclusive. Incidentally, the short-story writer also enjoys a game of cards with his friends (friends: source of inspiration, potential readers, help in time of need, and so on. Quite indispensable, friends are. And so are recreational activities; as a matter of fact, the short-story writer does some gardening every day to promote mental health. If it weren't for this hobby of his, the emotional stress would be unbearable!).

As it turns out after all this calculation, short-story writer Caio is left with two hours per day. He could, therefore, produce one short story per day. And herein lies the *problem*: Will half of this short story be bad, one quarter so-so, and one quarter good. Or will he produce, perhaps, one good short story every four days? In this case, could the days of the bad short stories be spent on something else—on meditation, for instance?

So, that's the problem. The short-story writer spends at least two hours a day turning this matter over in his mind.

Short-story writer Valfredo, a taxi driver, installed a tape recorder in his taxi. While driving, he would dictate short stories. Some of the passengers were frightened and wanted to get out of the car; others listened with interest, and some even made suggestions: "Make the woman kill the son!" Short-story writer Valfredo had problems of his own, too. A rival short-story writer, a traffic cop, fined him several times for driving recklessly. As a matter of fact, short-story writer Valfredo had been involved in accidents but according to him, they were caused by the car itself (brakes in poor condition) rather than by literature. Whatever the reason, the insurance agents wouldn't have anything to do with him and it was only through sheer perseverance that short-story writer Valfredo kept writing.

"You're a frustrated short-story writer!" Guilherme was yelling at me. "You lack form, you lack content, you lack everything!"

Me? And what about short-story writer Sílvio, who would tear up a short story as soon as he was half-way through and start a new one? Rumor had it that he didn't even know how to end a short story; I, however, being far less spiteful than Guilherme, would spread among the short-story writers the information that Sílvio certainly knew how to end a short story but he was very clever—by leaving it unfinished, he could always experience the joy of new things. Short-story writer Matias, not knowing what to write about, produced a short story consisting of incoherent sentences. It was rejected by all publishers. "It's stream of consciousness," Matias would say, indignant. "Why is Joyce's stream of consciousness considered good, but mine isn't? What's the difference? Is it because I'm Brazilian?" The short-story writers wouldn't reply to his questions; embarrassed, they averted their eyes.

At the age of eight, short-story writer Miguel wrote about nymphomaniacs. Short-story writer Rosemberg gave his sentences a special cadence, reminiscent of waltzes or tangos, as the case may be. Short-story writer Augusto, very involved in political concerns, went to a students' convention, where he watched the young people and took notes. The students, suspecting his motives, beat him up.

Short-story writer Vasco would take words from Guimarães Rosa's work and reshape them. Critic Valdo uncovered the following about short-story writer Marco: all his characters always had five-letter names, the second letter was always A, the last

one always O, with the stress falling on the first
syllable: Marco, Tarso, Lauro. Short-story writer
Paulo wrote only in the morning, when he merely
transcribed the dreams of the night before.

Short-story writer Norberto and short-story writer
Geraldo stood chatting on the street when they
witnessed the following scene: A lady was crossing
the street with a child in her arms. A car driving at
high speed appears. The driver tries to brake the car,
without success. The lady manages to throw the
child on the sidewalk, but she herself is struck down
and crushed by the car.

"Write a short story about it," said short-story
writer Norberto.

Short-story writer Geraldo wrote the following:

"Short-story writer Norberto and short-story writer
Geraldo stood chatting on the street when they
witnessed the following scene: A lady is crossing the
street with a child in her arms. A car driving at high
speed appears. The driver tries to brake the car,
without success. The lady manages to throw the
child on the sidewalk, but she herself is struck down
and crushed by the car."

"Are you trying to pull my leg?" asked short-
story writer Norberto when he finished reading.

"Yeah," said short-story writer Geraldo.

They laughed but soon fell silent and parted company without saying a word.

Imaginary news items. "The life of a short-story
writer can be filled with fun. Here at this moment
some short-story writers are showing us the pleasant
intimacy of an afternoon of autographs . . ."

Descriptions. Short-story writer Vasco, tall and thin.
Short-story writer Simão, short and fat. Short-story
writer Jan, tall and fat. Short-story writer Aurélio,
thin (at the age of eighteen) and fat (at the age of
twenty-nine). Details: Lalo's hooked nose. My mustache. My eyeglasses. The gait of some people, the

clothes of others, the laughter of this one here, the hair of that one there.

Short-story writer Antonio has native Indian blood. He wrote tragicomic stories about the aborigines. A tribal chief came to see him: "Why do you ridicule us? Haven't we had enough suffering already? Isn't it enough that our lands have been taken away from us? That we are stricken with tuberculosis? Do you still feel the need to make everybody laugh at us?" The tribal chief misunderstood my work, said short-story writer Antonio, chagrined. The Indians I talk about are not real, they are the Indians we have inside us. In our hearts we all wear ornamental feathers and G-strings.

Short-story writer Ramón wrote a series of stories about an imaginary country in Central America, called Cuenca. It had a dictator, large feudal landowners, a rising middle-class, a national liberation front whose members were arrested and tortured. Short-story writer Ramón, who lived in the United States, succeeded in having his book published. It sold well. A crafty entrepreneur made a bundle by raising money for Cuencan refugees.

Short-story writer Rômulo satirized his hometown in his writing. A mayor once kicked him out of town, but his successor requested that the writer return and then awarded him the Medal of Tourist Merit.

Short-story writer Sidney never used swear words in his short stories. He was afraid he might offend his aunt, an old nun.

Short-story writer Humberto, an algebra teacher, conceived the short story as a mathematical model. Short-story writer Ramião transcribed his own extrasensorial experiences.

Short-story writer John Sullivan wrote a series of stories published under the title *1997, After the Atomic War.* One hundred copies were placed in a radiation-proof shelter.

Short-story writer Ramsés said that there was more to a short story than just words; it should also include evidence of the circumstances under which it had been generated. To his book he affixed bus tickets of the buses in which he had shaped his short stories while traveling; movie tickets; bits and pieces of clothes; and even scraps of food. "I'm a wretched tailor," said short-story writer Newton, "but in my short stories I destroy villages and towns."

"It has just occurred to me that that tree in my short story is actually me," short-story writer Macário said to his lover at two o'clock in the morning. "What tree? What short story?" she muttered. She, too, was a short-story writer, but she suffered from insomnia, had difficulty falling asleep, and hated being wakened.

"I've been thinking a great deal about the meaning of my short stories," wrote elderly short-story writer Douglas in his journal, a notebook bound in leather. He always kept it under his pillow; if he were to die in his sleep, it wouldn't be hard for someone to find it and have it published.

Guilherme was grabbing at me, I was ready to pick a fight with him. Ramiro came over to restrain me. He seized the opportunity to inform me that thirty-eight copies of his book had already been sold, and his wife's relatives weren't even there yet: "It'll go as high as eighty, you'll see! Eighty!"

One day I took it into my head that short-story writers aren't writers at all: they are characters. I started thinking about a short story called "The Short-Story Writers." It would be my last one, I promised myself. But it wouldn't remain unpublished, oh no, it wouldn't; I'd see to it that it got published.

Every short story is a plea for help, short-story
writer Nicolau used to say. A resident of Green
Island, he would stuff the most anguished of his short
stories into bottles, which he would then hurl into
the river. "Maybe the fishermen will understand me,"
he would say to his wife.

Short-story writer Wenceslau said to his wife, a
beautiful brunette: "I'm sure that if you were to
have a talk with the editor, he would publish my
book, Morena. I'm sure he would, Morena."

Short-story writer Olívio, who worked with me at
the newspaper, was responsible for the trivia column. Surreptitiously he began to introduce his short
stories into the column: "Did you know that . . .
Adelaide, married to a French language teacher and
the lover of short-story writer Milton, has a dream in
which she sees the moon, split into two parts, fall off
the sky?" He was also considering the possibility of
writing short stories in the form of crossword puzzles.

Short-story writer Benjamin, a civil servant, would
report on a file of papers in a case by writing a
short story: "João M. Guimarães urgently requests the
overdue payments for the year 1965. I can imagine
João M. Guimarães in his small wooden house. . . ."
He was severely admonished by his boss, also a
short-story writer, who, however, never fiddled away
the hours when at work.

The inventive short-story writer Jane was contem-
plating the possibility of transmitting her short
stories via the telephone: "Hello! I'm short-story
writer Jane. I'm now going to read you one of my
short stories."

Short-story writer Misael intended to write brief
short stories in smoke up in the sky, using a
squadron of airplanes for this purpose.

Short-story writer Reginaldo had an inspiration: He
would write a short story in the form of an epitaph.
He started to scrutinize his friends, trying to detect in
them signs of some serious disease.

Seeing that her book *Efflorescence* wasn't selling, short-story writer Bárbara had a boy steal it from the bookstores for a sum of money. Over forty copies were stolen in a month and *Efflorescence* became third on the Best Sellers List.

Short-story writer Pedroso introduced the notion of efficiency into his literary production. His short stories were systematically rejected by newspapers and magazines; so, he had *Leviathan* published at his own expense and then hired the services of a specialized firm to conduct a public opinion poll. "How much has *Leviathan* changed your life?" was one of the questions posed to groups A, B, and C, to both men and women, to both blacks and whites. He intended to prove that his short stories were effective and that editors had a grudge against him. Unfortunately, the results of the poll were inconclusive.

Short-story writer Luís Ernesto would mimeograph his short stories, which he would then hand out at the gates of soccer stadiums; short-story writer Múcio painted short stories on Chinese vases.

Short-story writer Teodoro had his youngest son write to the program "The Little Box of Knowledge" requesting information on short-story writer Teodoro and the short stories he had written. The boy didn't get a reply because he had failed to enclose a Moko label with his letter.

Short-story writer Sezefredo lifted the prescription pad of his friend, Doctor Raul; then he forged a certificate stating that he suffered from an incurable disease. With this piece of paper in hand, he went from editor to editor, trying to get his book published: It's my last wish, he would say.

Short-story writer Rafael (Rafa). During the day he worked as a sales representative for a small appliances company; at night he wrote. Unable to find an editor willing to publish his book, he turned to his job with a vengeance. He ended up rich. Then he bought a publishing house, a printing shop, and had his book printed. He also bought several bookstores, whose store windows displayed dozens of copies of his book. Even so, the book didn't sell. . . . Short-story writer Rafa then began to give out free copies of his book to the schools; and he awarded scholarships to any student who learned his book by heart.

There was quite a hullabaloo in the bookstore. A salesclerk was accusing short-story writer Rodolfo of stealing a book.

"Me? Why would I want to steal a book?" Rodolfo was shouting. "And a book written by short-story writer Afranio at that! Everybody knows that Afranio and I are sworn enemies. Ramiro! Hey, Ramiro! Come over here, man! Tell this ass of a salesclerk what I think of Afranio's short stories. Come on, Ramiro! You can tell him that I . . . Come on, man, say it! I'll back you up! I will, Ramiro! You know me!"

Rodolfo was led away. While being dragged out of the store, he shouted:

"You bastards, you've torn my leather jacket! You accuse me of theft and on top of it you tear my jacket!"

It was true, his jacket had been torn. And Rodolfo was proud of that jacket of his, which made him feel, it was said, a Hemingway, a García Marquez.

This incident upset the short-story writers. Groups of them clustered together in the corners of the bookstore, where they stood whispering. Every so often, a short-story writer would detach himself from a group and walk over to another group, smoking and gesticulating.

On the whole, the short-story writers present there were young. Many had big brown eyes. On their faces one could see: anguish, despair, a need for greater participation, concern for social tensions, acute awareness of existential problems. Money was being discussed, and what is money? wondered one of them, while another smiled. I began looking for Marisa, in real earnest this time, but all I could see were books, short-story writers, and problems.

Problems. Short-story writer Arnulfo, married, the father of five children, found it impossible to get a moment of peace and quiet at home. It occurred to him that he should build a studio of sorts at the far end of his backyard. It took short-story writer Arnulfo, working Saturdays and Sundays, three years to finish the job. Then his oldest son asked him permission to use the place as a repair shop where he could fix home appliances. After giving much thought to his son's request, he finally gave his consent. My son is young, and I'm old, he would explain to his fellow short-story writers. Besides, the future of electronics is bright. . . . As for the short story, who knows?

Problems. Short-story writer Fischer wrote in a trancelike condition, when he scrawled away in big letters. His secretary (Fischer was the director of a publicity agency) typed out the originals. Fischer suspected that she added passages of her own but he had no proof that she actually did so.

Short-story writer Nepocumeno's problem was quite different. Not knowing how to type, he hired an excellent typist on a monthly basis at a high salary. She typed his work quickly; the short-story writer's output wasn't enough to keep her busy; the young woman was idle for long periods of time. Seeing his money draining away, he fired her. She went to the Ministry of Labor, brought an action against him, and the court ruled in her favor.

Short-story writer Plínio had an interesting problem, too. Once when he was alone at home, he was struck by a bright idea for a short story. Just then there was a power failure. There was no flashlight, nor candles, nor matches, nothing. Groping about, short-story writer Plínio managed to find a pen and a sheet of paper and he began to write a short story in the dark. He never succeeded (unlike short-story writer Fischer) in deciphering what he had written but he still has this sheet of paper, which he has saved with great care. Whatever this piece of writing is all about, one thing is sure: it is *not* a short story called "The Short-Story Writers."

Problems. Short-story writer Amílcar was kidnapped by five individuals who got out of a black car. He was taken to an empty house and for a week he was forced to write two short stories a day. Afterward, Amílcar saw those short stories published, under different names, in magazines and literary supplements.

As part of a development plan for the town of Ibirituiçá, its mayor, Macário, invited various short-story writers to take up residence there. He thought it would be a good way of promoting the town. However, when the few tourists who got there saw the short-story writers strolling in the main public square or sitting in the verandahs of old houses, where they were busy typing or writing in longhand, they were disappointed. The mayor, too, was disappointed and after taking legal action to have the short-story writers evicted, he repossessed the houses that had been granted to them.

Another problem. Short-story writer David wrote a series of historical short stories about the Italian settlements. For months he researched the subject in the libraries of the hinterland, wrote down testimonies, took pictures. "In your short stories," he was asked, "which parts are real, and which parts are fictional?" He didn't know, as he had lost the briefcase containing all the evidence he had gathered. Short-story writer Ofélia had to have sex with her husband soon after finishing a short story. When he happened to be away traveling, she found it impossible to write and considered being unfaithful to him. Short-story writer Gervásio wrote obscure short stories, which he showed to his girlfriends, promising to marry the one who understood them. None of them did. Short stories and women kept accumulating in the life of Gervásio.

Short-story writer Pereira . . . Now, that's a good one! Short-story writer Pereira once stopped writing when he was halfway through a short story. He couldn't come up with the right word. His wife suggested that he flip through the dictionary: I'm sure, she said, that when you chance upon the word you've been trying to find, it'll hit you like a seizure, you'll be thrilled, you'll be on cloud nine. The short-story writer rejected her suggestion. He thought it wouldn't be fair. It would be like a surgeon who had to look up things in a book in order to perform surgery, he explained.

She went ahead and bought a dictionary and started some research of her own. She would write down the more suggestive words on pieces of paper, which she would put in the bathroom, or on the coffee table. Pereira would tear them up without reading. When she reached the end of the dictionary, she left him.

The waiter walks by with a tray of empty glasses. "Waiter," I say, "I've got plenty of problems." He smiles at me, sympathetic. I feel encouraged.

"Waiter, let's see if you're smart enough to know the answer to this: If a short-story writer consumes eight hundred and twenty cubic centimeters of whiskey, how many cubic centimeters would twenty-eight short-story writers consume?"

The man eyes me suspiciously and wants to get away. I grab him by the arm:

"If eight short-story writers weigh five hundred

and seventy kilograms, how many kilograms does
one short-story writer weigh? And if you add
two hundred and seventy-one short-story writers to
four hundred and twenty-nine short-story writers,
how much does it amount to?"

I've offended the waiter. I can see I have. I'll make
it up to him by befriending him.

"Waiter . . ." I whisper in his ear. "This girl . . .
this Marisa . . . what a body she has, out of this
world. . . ."

Then a sudden misgiving:

"What if she writes short stories, too?"

In one of his short stories, short-story writer
Leandro compares the face of a young woman to a
cloud; in another, he compares a cloud to the face of
a young woman.

Short-story writer Frederico, believing that his
short stories should have something practical about
them, refused to use metaphors; instead, his
writing was interspersed with the proverbs of La
Rochefoucauld. He used to say that any idiot could
write a short story using the first person narrator.

"I'll have to avoid this kind of mistake in 'The
Short-Story Writers,' " I mumble.

All of a sudden, I'm all fired up. "The Short
Story-Writers"! What a short story! It will consist of
a succession of cameos, there will be a multitude of
characters revealed by quick flashes—a Woodstock
of the short story! A short story of a book! Bound to
have repercussions, no doubt about it. Will it?

After the publication of her book, short-story
writer Malvina sent anonymous letters to every
newspaper. "Malvina has invigorated literature," she
stated in one of the letters. "She is dynamic," she
wrote in another, "gentle," in yet another.

Short-story writer Victor put together an anthology of unknown short-story writers. The collection was well received by the critics. Many years later, short-story writer Victor revealed that he was the author of every single short story in it.

And now for the tricks!

Short-story writer Manoel wrote letters, such as the following, to American writers:

Dear Mr. Roth,

Below is a list of my most recently written short stories, and at the prices quoted, they are available to you for immediate delivery.

"The Discovery" (US$15.00). Gilberto and Paulo, old friends, find out that they are homosexual. A great shock to both of them. Three dramatic, yet exciting, situations, each one a paragraph long.

"Specks" (US$13.80). Alberto knows that painting is his vocation, but he has to look after his father's farm. A violent conflict: the father, hemiplegic but domineering. A detailed account of the problem of the arts in an underdeveloped country. The sinister figure of a *marchand de tableaux*.

Untitled (US$9.90). A long story, but with an impressive unity of time: one single night. A group of intellectuals discusses national and world issues. Intoxicants are present. Deep introspection.

In addition to the short stories listed above, there are also four others in various stages of completion.

Yours truly, etc., etc.

Short-story writer Zeferino was very afraid of baring his soul in his short stories. And yet he was terribly autobiographical. He solved the problem, at least in part, by using a simple trick: He narrated the

events in the life of his mother as if they had
happened to his father; and the things that had
actually happened to the writer himself, he would
ascribe to his sister.

The waiter walks by, this time the glasses are full.
I run after him. Short-story writer Mateus accosts me:
    "Have you met my daughter?"
    A beautiful girl, blond, with green eyes.
    "Are you going to be a short-story writer too, my
child?" I ask.
    "She's into writing already," informs her mother
proudly.
    "Writing must run in the family," I remark.
    "What about you, what are you writing?" asks
Mateus.
    "A short story called 'The Short-Story Writers.' "
    "Ah," says Mateus. He gathers his family round
him and hurries away.
    Meanwhile, the waiter has disappeared. I loiter
about, watching the other short-story writers. They
chat, tell stories, narrate the extraordinary adventures
they have been through.
    Short-story writer Ronny rips the cover from each
book of short stories that he reads; he plasters the
walls of his bedroom with them; however, the book
covers are not properly glued and they flutter with a
soft rustling sound in the evening breeze that comes
in through the window. Short-story writer Ronny
claims that in this faint noise he can hear the voices of
the short-story writers mumbling their short stories,
but nobody believes him, they laugh at this nonsense.
    Whenever short-story writer Aderbal got home, he
would phone his editor to ask him how many
copies of his book had been sold that day. Not one,
the answer invariably was. Uttering a swear word,
the short-story writer would hang up. He would then
ask the housemaid if there were any messages. Yes,

one—requesting him to go to a certain address to do a special job. With a sigh, the short-story writer would pick up a small black suitcase; taking a taxi, he would go to the given address. A beautiful house. He would ring the bell and a man, fat and diffident, would open the door.

"You can call me Alberto," the man would say. "Follow me this way, please."

He would lead the short-story writer to a bedroom, where a blond, middle-aged woman, not very attractive, would be lying in bed. She would be wearing a pink nightgown and would smile shyly. The short-story writer would look at her carefully, then would open the small suitcase from which he would take out a transmitter, earphones, and microphones.

"Where should I stay?" the man would ask.

"As far away as possible, Alberto. In the large hall, for instance."

Alberto would fit a set of headphones over his ears, clutch one of the microphones, and disappear. Short-story writer Aderbal would wait for a while and then begin to test the sound equipment:

"Testing, testing. Hello, Alberto."

"Hello," would reply the voice at the other end of the line. A voice that almost cracked.

"Okay, Alberto."

Then, lying down alongside the woman, his eyes fixed on her, the short-story writer would begin to speak into the microphone:

"Her eyes are as blue as the lakes in the Alps."

The woman would draw closer to him.

"Her hair is like silk."

"And her arms?" The man's voice would echo anxiously in the headphones.

"Take it easy, Alberto. Her arms . . . Her arms are nicely shaped, perfect. Like alabaster."

"Like what?"

"Alabaster, Alberto. Alabaster. It's used in chandeliers."

"Ah."

"Alabaster skin, with delicate blue veins."

"Oh, my God," Alberto would moan. "I never . . . And her legs?"

"Like two fish moving about in tepid waters, two elongated fish."

"Ah, you don't say! And tell me now: her small boobs?"

"Just a moment."

After a pause:

"Like two little fawns."

"But isn't this from the *Song of Songs*?" Alberto would ask, suspicious.

"So what? Just because something has been said before doesn't make it invalid."

Another pause.

"And her belly?" Alberto would ask.

There would be no reply.

"And her belly? Hello. Hello! And her belly?"

"One moment . . . Just a moment, one short moment . . ."

"And her belly? What about her belly?"

"Ah . . ."

"Hello?"

"Yes. Her belly. Now yes. Her belly is like a sea of placid waters. . . ."

"Oh . . ."

Another pause.

"Wait for three minutes, then you can come in," Aderbal would announce in a neutral tone of voice.

The man would come in, look first at the woman, who would be facing the wall, then at the short-story writer, who would be putting the equipment back into the small suitcase.

"I'll be darned. . . . Gosh . . . Imagine . . . I never . . . How much do I owe you?"

"Three hundred."

"Money well spent," the man would say, writing

out a check. "You know, I also dabble at writing short stories. Would you care to . . . ?"

"Sorry," Aderbal would say. "Not my specialty. Get a literary critic. Good-bye."

Once out in the street, he would run toward the first phone booth that he saw, then dial the editor's number: Had any copies of his book been sold yet? Nope. Aderbal would return home.

Short-story writers might be aggressive, but they are harmless. In World War I a battalion of short-story writers was decimated; an inspection of their rifles revealed that not a single bullet had been fired. Short-story writers are hard to digest. A tribe of cannibals once devoured an entire expedition of short-story writers; the cannibals became sick and suffered from hallucinations during which they kept telling endless stories.

From Stockholm, a friend of short-story writer Emílio once sent him the following telegram written in Swedish: "We inform you that you've been selected for the Nobel prize for literature. Be in Stockholm on the tenth." When somebody translated the telegram for him, short-story writer Emílio laughed his head off, but later he was torn by nagging doubts. And on the night between the ninth and the tenth, he didn't get a wink of sleep. On the following morning, the winner of the Nobel prize was announced, and it wasn't short-story writer Emílio. It's a literary clique, he said, piqued.

Castaway on a deserted island, short-story writer Carmosino had nothing but his manuscripts; however, it was thanks to them that he managed to survive.

He attracted the fish to the shore by throwing scraps of paper into the water; he caught the fish with fishhooks made from the paper clips that had held the short stories together. The bait? Paper pellets. For some reason, the fish went for them.

Using a few sheets of paper, the short-story writer would start a fire with the help of the sun shining through the lenses of his eyeglasses. He ate broiled fish.

He also built a paper shed and with the only blank sheet of paper he made a small flag that, hoisted up a tall pole, proved to be his salvation: He was seen and rescued. While on board the ship, he asked for paper and pen and immediately hurled himself into the task of reconstructing his short stories.

Short-story writer Morton, a missionary, lived for many years in Africa, among the Pygmies. He wrote a great deal, but there was nobody to whom he could show his short stories: the barbarians didn't like him. As Morton related in his memoirs: "I would ask God to send me a person willing to read one of my short stories. Just one single short story would do. And he wouldn't have to express an opinion, just read it. One single reader is enough to save a short-story writer." Short-story writer Efraim became a hippie, built a tree house on top of a fig tree and there he spent his days writing short stories. The tree had to be cut down to save him from starving himself to death.

Short-story writer Franz regarded himself as a man who hadn't had much life experience (his short stories were purely introspective). Bent on seeing the world, he boarded a Norwegian freighter. Eight years later, he was one of the best stokers in the Atlantic. He still wrote, but only letters to his family. The characters created by short-story writer Helena, a manicurist, were fingernails: "I write about what I know," she would say.

And what about closet short-story writers?

A young acquaintance of mine is apprenticed to a printer.

Although intelligent and hard-working, he hasn't been successful in his effort to master the craft. Throughout the day he has a run of bad luck: he bumps into the machines, spills ink, overturns the galleys. He is the laughingstock of his fellow workers. And the owner of the print shop, a grouchy man, is always taking him to task.

I know this print shop, which is located in a distant neighborhood. It's in an old house, dismal-looking and isolated: All the neighboring houses are being torn down to make room for a wide tree-lined street.

I can imagine this area at night. The moon shines upon what is left of the walls. The street, covered with potholes, is deserted.

It is then that the printer's devil appears. Wrapped up in an old cape, he walks fast. He arrives at the print shop; he glances around him to make sure he is alone; he inserts something resembling a hook into the keyhole. There is some maneuvering, a click, the door opens, and zap! He is inside, puffing. He lights a candle—just one. He doesn't dare have more light, even though he knows he is alone.

Taking off his cape, he gets down to work: He turns on the machines, he melts down the lead. And he turns his full attention to the linotype.

Hours of strenuous work.

What does the apprentice write as he practices his craft? Well, things that pop into his head, phrases, stories . . .

Short stories.

Short stories! He writes short stories. Are these short stories any good? What if they are very good? What if the printer's devil happens to be the best short-story writer in the country?

I would like to see his writing revealed to the world. Unfortunately there's nothing I can do about this.

While I stand pondering the matter, the printer's devil toils on. Before his supervisor he is slow, but the solitude of dawn endues unsuspected deftness. Sentences sprout quickly in his brain, but his fingers, even swifter, involuntarily devise protagonists, situations.

And if I were to have a word with the owner of the print shop? I'm not sure. . . . I don't know him; besides, I'm afraid I'm no good at persuading a pragmatic, inflexible man.

Maybe with the help of the authorities . . . An anonymous letter to the police. "Suspicious activities have been observed in print shop X in the small hours." The authorities would go to the place, catch the apprentice red-handed, confiscate his short stories. And if the youth is indeed as good a short-story writer as I suspect he is, his short stories would surely make an impression on some police clerk or newspaperman, who would then take it upon themselves to show the short stories to an editor brave enough to take a chance on them. As for the legal complications rising from the act of breaking into the print shop, from the work done after hours—well, who would bother with such things if the book became a success?

While I formulate hypotheses, the printer's devil makes haste. He doesn't want to be caught there by the rising sun! With brazenness, he now works at full tilt.

Finally the book is finished. It is a beautiful volume of two hundred and twenty pages, containing five long short stories and twenty-two short short stories. It doesn't have a title; it's an experimental piece of work.

The printer's devil stands up, stretches, rubs his congested eyes. Listlessly, he leafs through the book. Yawning, he opens the furnace—and hurls it into the flames!

The next half hour is spent tidying up. He cleans and sweeps up until everything is orderly. When he is finished, the print shop looks exactly as he found it. After casting one last glance around him, he snuffs out the candle and leaves. He goes home. Where does he live? I don't know.

What I do know, however, is that tomorrow he'll write another book. That's what short-story writers are like.

Short-story writer Herman carried out two kinds of experiments: One involved a singer who emitted a high note capable of shattering a crystal glass; the other involved newly formed words. About the singer, he found out that the shattering of the crystal was caused by the particular vowel she had chosen rather than by the highness and intensity of the sound—and this vowel happened to be Herman's favorite. As for the newly formed words, Herman found out that when these words were combined with that particular vowel, the vibrations they emitted were so powerful that they rocked the very foundations of buildings and bridges.

"My God!" murmured Herman in his study. "Such is the power of words!"

Despite his friends' insistence, he refused to reveal these words. His friends kept bugging him so much that he finally promised to utter the words after he retired; but he died before his retirement.

Sitting on the floor, I notice a sausage under a bookcase; I'm going to pick it up; however, I think better of it. "The cockroaches need it more than I do," I mumble disdainfully. Short-story writer Kafka, now there's a guy who liked cockroaches.

I found myself unable to get to my feet. What the devil, I muttered.

The devil? The devil.

Rumor has it that the devil had an appointment with mediocre short-story writer Neto; they were to meet at the city's cemetery. There, at midnight, the evil one presented the following option to the short-story writer: another forty years of life and bad literature—or one single outstanding short story, the best ever written, to be followed by death one minute after the completion of the last sentence. Without the slightest hesitation, short-story writer Neto opted for the second alternative. The contract was signed in blood, etc., and the devil told him to go home and start writing; his hand would be guided throughout the composition of the precious lines.

However, as he was leaving the cemetery, the short-story writer was killed after being run over by a hearse. Afterward the devil disclaimed responsibility for the accident; the hearse belonged to the local parish and was therefore in the service of God.

"The Short-Story Writers." What a short story! I dispensed with all kinds of rituals—short-story writer Lucio's ritual or anyone else's. I didn't have to fortify myself with a drink before I started working, neither was there any need for me to crease my brow as I sat down at the typewriter. As a matter of fact, I wrote "The Short-Story Writers" as I lay down, motionless; my eyes would follow the words that appeared on the ceiling of my bedroom (that's how the short-story writer produced a very abbreviated short story on the wall of Nebuchadnezzar's palace for his reader Daniel). At first the words emerged one by one; soon they came in sentences and paragraphs flashing by so swiftly that I could follow them only by speed reading. I was open-mouthed with astonishment. The short story was in the process of being written!

Struggling short-story writers. Short-story writer Lauro went hungry and yet he lent money to short-story writer Antonio so that he could have a book of his published. Short-story writers Rudimar, Heráclito, and Costa were thinking of starting up a writers' cooperative. Short-story writer Breno dreamed of a farm where all short-story writers would live a communal life, milking cows and plowing fields in the morning, and writing in the afternoon. He even considered setting up a print shop where the writers themselves would do all the work. The profits would go to a common fund. Short-story writer Paulo and his brother, a photographer, worked in a park. The photographer blew up photographs to poster size and the short-story writer wrote a two-page short story about the person in the photograph. Short-story writers João, Lino, and Amílcar wrote a six-handed short story. Each one wrote one line. Before starting, they decided that the total number of lines would be a multiple of three.

Four short-story writers decided to beat up literary critic Arthur. One night they went to this Arthur's house. Four strong, tall young men walked abreast in silence, their footsteps echoing on the deserted street. "Just like in the Old West," murmured one of them. Five short-story writers about to part company tore a short story into five pieces. Each one of them left with one piece. Thirty short-story writers made a pact: They would read each other's short stories to the end of their lives.

"Marisa!" I shout, but the book-filled shelves muffle my voice.

Daily, upon waking up, short-story writer Firmo murmured: "I'm a short-story writer, I'm a short-story writer." And he felt better.

The bookstore emptied gradually. Outside, pedestrians carrying briefcases hurried by, wrapped in their grey overcoats. They looked at us and wondered: Who are they?

"We're short-story writers," I bellowed, and pummeled myself on the head: "Are you nuts, short-story writer?"

The mother of Absalão, the crazy short-story writer, took him to a psychologist who practiced in the neighborhood.

"Listen carefully," said the psychologist, "I'm going

to say something absurd. A man was found with
his feet tied up. And with his hands tied up behind his
back. It is believed that he tied himself up."
Absalão remains silent.
"The man's feet," went on the psychologist, carefully watching the short-story writer, "were so huge
that in order to take off his pants he had to pull them
over his head."
Absalão still silent. The psychologist:
"A skull was found in an old grave in Spain. It was
Christopher Columbus's, at the age of ten."
"Such marvelous stories, doctor!" shouted Absalão,
amazed. Drawing out paper and pen, he proceeded
to write them down.
Short-story writer Garcia read his short stories to
his psychiatrist. When paying for his treatment, he
demanded that he be given a discount for the time he
had spent reading aloud; he even thought he should
receive a token payment, arguing that, if his short
stories were available in books, the doctor would
have to pay for them.
Short-story writer Jesualdo, a medical student,
lifted case histories from textbooks and then had
them published as short stories. Short-story writer
Baltazar, a psychiatric nurse, read his short stories to
his patients. He believed that by doing so, he improved their condition. "The more depressing the
short stories are, the better the patients feel."

Ramiro eyes me rancorously. I'm spoiling the best
afternoon of his life. I'm a despicable bastard, I say to
myself, hiccupping. What's the matter with me?

A short-story writer complained to his doctor
about being unable to write. X-rays were taken but
nothing abnormal was found. Short-story writer
Nélio wrote incessantly. His short stories described

something insignificant that grew and grew, spilling over into the house, the city; a mouse was transformed into a thirty-ton rat; excrement piled up mountain high; a person's left ear was changed into a wing two meters in diameter. While writing, short-story writer Nélio didn't pay attention to the small tumor that kept growing near his nose.

Short-story writer Bárbara tells about a short-story writer who is almost killed when a bookshelf comes crashing down upon him. The books were written by the short-story writer himself, who then gives up writing.

Short-story writer Hildebrando, a flight attendant, was on board a plane that caught fire during a crash landing. Passengers say that he acted bravely; he only stopped looking after them when the captain announced that they were about to land. Then, drawing a notebook out of his pocket, he began to write. Later, his wife read in the scorched notebook: "Idea for a short story: R., a rich banker, is on board an airplane that . . ." The sentence was unfinished. That's the way it was printed in Hildebrando's posthumous book.

Short-story writer Amélio was the subject of a photographic study. A Praktisix camera with a 180mm lens was used with an aperture opening of f/5.6, an exposure time of 1/125, and Tri-X Kodak film. Some remarkable details of these photographs: the whites of the eyes—the creased forehead—the fingers crimped over the keyboard of the typewriter—the rictus of the mouth. The untimely death of short-story writer Amélio increased the value of these photographs.

Short-story writer Miro, who suffered from cerebral arteriosclerosis, had difficulty coming up with the right words for his short stories. He would then leave blank spaces in his sentences, hoping to fill them in later when memory came to his aid. His last short stories had many blank pages.

While suffering the pains of a renal colic, short-story writer Ibrahim wrote an inspired short story. . . . Short-story writer Peter broke a leg and wrote a short story on the cast. . . . Short-story writer Alfredo was cross-eyed; short-story writer Elizabeth suffered from generalized lupus erythematosus. "What would you do if you had only one hour to live?" a reporter asked short-story writer Matos. "I would do what has to be done: I would write a short story." "Would it be a pessimistic short story?" "Not necessarily." "And would one hour be enough to write it?" "Maybe yes, maybe no."

In the last days of his life, short-story writer Salomão wrote effortlessly. He didn't even have to think: The phrases kept sprouting spontaneously. "I'm pure literature," he would say. He looked translucent because of the leukemia.

Marisa has left, there's nothing else for me to do, except gymnastics. I take hold of two thick books and start doing arm lifts. They take the books away from me. They, who? The short-story writers. But death will catch up with them.

Short-story writer Martim said: "There are more cars for people to drive than there are pedestrians for drivers to run over, more people who write than people who read—this is the portrait of our times." Short-story writer Raimundo: "Paper has become so expensive that we can no longer afford to write long short stories." Somebody phoned this same short-story writer to find out which stores sold his book. He refused to give out the information: "You'd be better off not buying it. There are at least two hundred other books on the market far better than mine." Short-story writer Barroso, a rich heir, did nothing but write, and he wouldn't accept any form

of payment for his short stories: "It's my way of
paying back to mankind the money I've inequitably
received," he would say. Short-story writer Limeira,
from the state of Acre, used to say: "Show me an
anthology that includes someone from Acre." He was
a very distrustful person and finally gave up literature.

Another person who gave up literature was short-
story writer Alberto. He opened a grocery store and
would say: "All of us have had a father and a mother,
all of us have been through childhood, we've been
traumatized, we've had affairs. Why in the world
should we get under everybody's skin by foisting
our short stories on them? Isn't it enough to have to
deal with life's daily worries, with taxes, with
expenses? I sell salami, which soothes the stomach."
Short-story writer Morais gave up writing to grow
roses and short-story writer Ymai to become a
terrorist. Short-story writer Murilo didn't give up
literature entirely: He opened a correspondence school
for writers. "In a month you will be able to write as
well as Guimarães Rosa," the brochures guaranteed.
Short-story writer Feijó systematically received re-
jection slips from publishers. He set his short stories
aside, established himself in the grain business, and
became rich. He then established the Feijó Literary
Prize, whose rules stipulated that the winning short
story would become the property of the Feijó Group.

When he got hold of the winning short story, Feijó
would tear it up, saying: I've just saved this short-
story writer from a painful career.

There were only a couple of us now—even
Ramiro had left—and the waiter had long since made
himself scarce. I felt it was time for me to go. I had
to finish a short story called "The Short-Story Writers."

Short-story writer Georgariou lived in an attic
and wrote at dusk. At that hour huge bats would fly

in through the open window and attack him vi-
ciously. The short-story writer did his best to defend
himself; but at times he became absent-minded and
the bats sucked his blood. Despite being anemic, the
short-story writer wrote incessantly.

Short-story writer Ronny . . . No, I've already
mentioned him.

Short-story writer Aristarco: "To live? Who? Me? I
live only to gather material for my short stories."

I labored up the stairs. Like short-story writer
Hawthorne, I could say: "Here I am, in my own
room. Here I have finished many short stories. It's a
bewitched place, haunted by thousands and thousands
of visions—some of which have now been made
visible to the world. Sometimes I felt as if I were
lying in a tomb, cold, motionless, bloated; sometimes I felt happy. . . . Now I begin to understand
why I have been imprisoned in this solitary room
for so many years, and why it was impossible for me
to tear down its invisible bars. Had I succeeded in
escaping, I would now be insensitive and harsh and
my heart would be covered with the dust of the
earth. . . . Truly, we are nothing but shadows."

"Shadows," I muttered. I pushed the door open
with my foot, testing my unsteady balance.

Marisa was there, lying on my bed, smoking.

"I dropped in to read this short story of yours," she
said. " 'The Short-Story Writers,' isn't it?"

It was.